A Twist of Love

Justice #5

Suzan Harden

This is a work of fiction. All characters, organizations and events in this novel are products of the author's imagination and are not to be construed as real. Any resemblance to persons, living or dead, is entirely coincidental.

A TWIST OF LOVE
(Justice #5)
ISBN-13 - 978-1-64918-001-8

Published by Angry Sheep Publishing
Findlay, Ohio

Cover Design by For the Muse Designs
Interior Design by QA Productions

More by Suzan Harden

Bloodlines

Blood Magick
Zombie Love
Zombie Confidential
Zombie Wedding
Amish, Vamps & Thieves
Blood Sacrifice
Love, War & a Bulldog
Zombie Goddess
Ravaged
Sacrificed
Reality Bites
Ghouls in the Grocery
Resurrected
Bloodlines Shorts Anthology

Seasons of Magick

Spring
Summer
Autumn
Winter
The Season of Magick Anthology

Justice

Sword and Sorceress 28 ("Justice")
Sword and Sorceress 30
("Diplomacy in the Dark")
Justice: The Beginning
A Question of Balance
A Modicum of Truth
A Matter of Death
A Touch of Mother
A Twist of Love
A Virtue of Child
A Hand of Father (Coming Soon)

The Justice Thalia Stories

Snowfall
Murder Most Fowl
The Sweetest Poison (Coming Soon)

888-555-HERO

Hero De Facto
Hero Ad Hoc
Hero De Novo
A Very Hero Christmas
Hero De Jure
Hero In Camera
Hero Amicus Curiae (Coming Soon)
A Very Hero Wedding (Coming Soon)
Hero Ad Litem (Coming Soon)

Millersburg Magick Mysteries

Spells and Sleuths
Fae and Felonies
Magick and Murder

Miscellaneous

Sword and Sorceress 31 ("Pig-Headed")
Sword and Sorceress 32 ("Unexpected")

For updates, news, and giveaways, join Suzan's mailing list or visit her website (www.suzanharden.com), Twitter, (@Suzan_Harden), or Facebook (SuzanHardenWriter).

Prologue

Love and Conflict were reunited when Love returned to the World at Mother's behest. Their twins Knowledge, that which is known by humans, and Thief, that which is unknown by humans, were born. However, such peace could not last. It was simply not in either Love or Conflict's natures.

With the new existence of Death, Conflict found Himself fascinated with Her. He sent Her the purest gold, the most exotic foods, and the rarest of Child's flowers to Her. While Death thanked Him for His gifts, She spurned His attempts to woo Her. He started wars in order to send Her the spirits of humans, their light to compliment Her magnificent darkness. Still, She would not lay with Him.

Conflict's obsession with Death did not go unnoticed by Love. Jealousy flooded Her once again. Love plotted to remove Death so Conflict's attention would return to Her once more.

Upon finding a woman close to dying, Love lay in wait for Death in the woman's hut. When Death entered the woman's abode to collect her spirit, Love stabbed Death in the heart with Her glittering knives.

"Oh, my dear sister," Death said as she pulled Love's knives free from Her breast. "You cannot kill that which is already dead. Why do You wish to harm Me?"

"You've taken Conflict Who is My own heart and soul," Love wailed.

"I have taken nothing from You." Death shook Her head sadly. "When

You created Conflict, You gave birth to His own will. Just as Balance did the same for Me."

Death stepped closer to Love and brushed the tears from Love's cheeks. "You, however, are quite lovely. Would You come with Me instead of this poor woman?" She gestured at the human lying in her bed, struggling to breathe.

Confused, Love asked, "Why would You want Me?"

Death smiled. "Because part of My purpose is to show the World why You are so special."

And so, Death took Love to Her realm.

—The Third Book of Love, Verses I thru XI

Chapter 1

I sat at my scarred oak desk in my office and stared at the pile of morning dispatches from the home Temple of Balance in Standora, the capital of the Queendom of Issura. Summer's heat was upon us even this early in the morning. Despite my office being located within the cool marble depths of my own Temple, I hadn't bothered with my formal robes. It was too warm.

So I perched on my chair in leggings and tunic, considering if taking my boots off was a move too close to breaking etiquette for my station, and I stared at the pile. There shouldn't be this many dispatches from Standora. Not during the height of the growing season.

My city of Orrin was the third largest city in Issura and its second largest port. Normally, we would only have our share of petty crime, property damage from brawling sailors, and the occasional stabbing when a brawl got out of hand before the city peacekeepers arrived to break it up.

But ever since I was assigned, or rather sentenced, as the city's chief justice a little over a year ago, it seemed like the Twelve decided to up the ante. Especially over the last six months. And I was hoping for, or dreading, some more information in today's dispatches about one problem in particular.

I ran my fingertips over the seals of the various pieces of parchments until I found the one with the personal sigil of the Reverend Mother herself. I cracked the wax and brushed my fingers over the raised symbols of the Temple of Balance to read them. Even though I was no longer totally blind like the rest of my sisterhood, I couldn't discern the difference between ink and parchment as sighted people did. There wasn't a large enough difference in the level of heat for me to read ink writing.

As I suspected she would but I desperately wished otherwise, the Reverend Mother failed to give me any more details about Gerd's escape from custody in Standora. I wanted to throw the tiny scroll across the room. Gerd, the former high sister of Orrin's Temple of Love, may be my birth mother, but she was insane and dangerous and on the loose.

Not necessarily in that order, and I was at the top of her list of people she wanted dead.

The Reverend Mother should have tried and executed Gerd months ago after she was discovered demon dealing among her multiple other crimes. Once again, the Reverend Mother failed to explain in her letter why Gerd was still alive, much less how the Mad Whore removed shackles designed to inhibit her magical talents, killed a warden and escaped from the capital. I crumpled the parchment and threw it anyway, knowing my senior clerk Donella would merely give me disapproving looks when she carefully smoothed it out and added it to the official records.

The wadded ball barely missed Sivan's head as she entered my office with my breakfast. I received the disapproving look earlier than expected. My personal assistant and head of household shoved aside some other documents with her elbow, set the tray on my desk, and turned to close the door.

"I'm sorry, Sivan," I said.

She bent to pick up the wadded parchment and examined the broken seal as she straightened. "I'm assuming you weren't happy with whatever the Reverend Mother said."

"More like her lack of saying anything," I grumbled. "Dragonfly has gotten more information from the Reverend Mother of Love than I have from Balance. If I didn't know better, I'd think my own Reverend Mother hopes Gerd will succeed in killing me this time around."

"I doubt it," Sivan said dryly. "She went to too much trouble to force you to be Orrin's chief justice." She carefully straightened the parchment I'd thrown and laid it on the pile of dispatches I hadn't read yet. "Not to mention, it's been over a month since Gerd escaped. She's a lot of things, but stupid isn't one of them. She probably hightailed it for the Gray Mountains. Get through those before the snows start, especially with a death sentence here."

"The Reverend Mother of Love seemed rather certain Gerd would head south to seek revenge," I said.

"As I just said, Gerd's—" Sivan started.

"Not stupid," I finished while I poured a cup of tea from the steaming ceramic pot on the tray. "But she makes less sense than a Wixáritari Wildling priestess using peyōtl."

Sivan shrugged. "Let's try a different subject. How long are you planning to mope about the Temple?"

"I am not moping," I said. "And definitely not about Gerd."

"You've been moping ever since you found out Sister Claudia is carrying High Brother Luc's child." Sivan folded her arms across her chest. "And it's gotten worse now that she's showing. You say you've accepted the edict—"

I leaned my elbows on my desk and propped my chin on my fists. "She asked me to attend the birth."

"Oh. Oh, dear." Sivan dropped into one of the visitor's chairs without my permission, but I didn't have the heart to chide her over the etiquette misstep.

Maybe I wanted someone to talk to about this situation. I couldn't talk to Yanaba. She was also pregnant thanks to the stupid edict.

I couldn't talk to Elizabeth either. She had been raped and tortured for nearly a year when the renegades secretly took over our sister city Tandor, so she had a special dispensation from Child excluding her from the order to procreate. Feeling pity for myself because I was barren seemed like a terrible thing to complain about to a friend and fellow justice who'd suffered so much.

And I'd been born barren and blind thanks to my birth mother's attempt to illegally abort me.

"What did you tell Claudia?" Sivan said softly.

"I tried to jest about it, saying we should see how I handle Yanaba's delivery first." I sighed. "I don't know what to do. Part of me hates her for giving Luc what I can't—"

"Stop right there." Sivan held up her right palm. "This isn't about what you want. Or even what Luc and Claudia want. They would never have lain together if it weren't for that damn edict."

"And the other, logical, part of me knows that. This is about breeding as many children with Light and Balance talent as we can." I groaned and laid my forehead on my desk. "What is wrong with me, Sivan?"

"Felicitations, Chief Justice. You've finally joined the human race."

I rolled my head to the side so I could look at her. "What's that supposed to mean?"

"You hold yourself, and everyone else around you, to impossible standards." Sivan shook her head. "As a result, you make yourself and everyone around you miserable."

I sat upright and glared at her. "Excuse me for trying to adhere—"

Someone banged on my office door. "Chief Justice Anthea!" my head warden Little Bear called out. Another round of banging as Sivan rose and opened the door.

"What the demon are you carrying on about?" she snapped.

He shot her a sheepish grin and whispered, "Sorry, m'love," before he turned to me and inclined his head. "I apologize for intruding before you've finished your first pot of tea, Chief Justice, but there's a messenger from Love who says it's quite urgent he speak to you."

"Send them in."

Little Bear gestured. It wasn't one of the stablehands or one of the priestesses' children as I expected. Ichik, Sister Claudia's personal assistant, appeared in the doorway. They wore the standard uniform of the staff of the Temple of Love, but their long hair was loose. Whatever had happened, they hadn't had a chance to do one of the intricate hairstyles the staff of Love were known for before rushing to Balance. They were also slightly out of breath.

Ichik bowed. "Please forgive the intrusion, Chief Justice, and my disarray. The high sister begs most urgently for your presence in her chambers."

The alarm rolling off the eunuch spiked a rush of my own nerves. Why hadn't Dragonfly sent her own personal assistant if it were that urgent to meet with me?

"What happened?" I rose and reached for my formal robes, sword and harness hanging from their pegs. "Is Dragonfly all right?"

"No, Lady Justice." Ichik's voice shook. "She is not all right. No one in the Temple of Love is. She asks that you come immediately." Between their fear and their loyalty to Dragonfly and Claudia, I wasn't going to get anything more out of them.

I glanced with longing at the steaming cup on my desk as I donned my gear. So much for having my first pot of Jing tea before disaster struck.

Sivan caught my yearning look. "I'll brew a fresh round for you when you return, m'lady."

Little Bear exited my office, and his bellow for Gina and Dezba echoed through the Temple corridors. The two female wardens were a better choice to accompany me. After the awful things Gerd and her cohorts had done to the sisters of Love, the priestesses had a tendency to draw weapons first and ask questions later when it came to armed men. The eunuchs that served them were barely tolerated right now as it was, despite the Temple of Child doing their best to heal the priestesses' spirits.

Gina and Dezba ran up to me as I entered the courtroom with Ichik trailing behind me. Balance didn't have a true sanctuary as the other eleven Temples did. The citizens didn't worship her. Balance meted out what a person deserved, and no amount of pleading or prayer swayed her. That was why her priestesses, like Yanaba, Elizabeth, and me, meted out judgement for wrongdoers and restitution for victims.

"Horses, m'lady?" Gina asked as I strode toward the main doors.

"No, it's not worth the time to saddle them, but let's give Dezba a moment to fix her attire." I raised an eyebrow as the young warden attempted to secure her padded leather jerkin. From her damp hair that was merely braided instead of pinned up like Gina's, Dezba had been rousted from her bath.

"My apologies, Lady Justice," she murmured as her skin went from orange to red while she struggled with the laces.

I shook my head. "If Ichik here had been half a candlemark earlier, I would be in the same position. However, we do have an image to maintain in public."

With Gina's assistance, Dezba was presentable within three breaths.

I exited through the main door with a nod to Warden Ahiga who stood guard, jogged down the marbles steps, and strode at a brisk clip toward the Temple of Love. My wardens and Ichik trailed behind me.

It was early enough in the morning that traffic was light on Orrin's main thoroughfare. A few people gave us curious looks, but for the most part everyone ignored us. It probably had something to do with my lecture to the citizens of Orrin last month about knowing when to mind their own business and knowing to speak up when they learned of an injustice.

It also meant there were fewer spies watching me these days.

When we reached the Temple of Love, Sister Shada met us in the foyer. She wasn't wearing her formal robes or veil. For a brief instant, I feared something may have happened to Claudia and her unborn child. But surely, Dragonfly would have sent for a master healer, not me.

Shada bowed. "This way, Chief Justice."

From the whispers of the other priestesses and servants, not everyone knew what was going on. Like Shada, none of the priestesses were dressed in their formal wear. It wasn't like Dragonfly or Claudia to keep secrets from the sisters either. My gut clenched as I matched Shada's pace back to the priestesses' private quarters.

Shada knocked softly on the door. Love's Chief Warden Citana opened the door to Dragonfly's bedchambers just enough to see who it was. Citana relaxed a bit when she saw me. Shada inclined her head to me.

"Call if you need additional assistance, Chief Justice." The silence as she walked away was unnerving. I was too used to the tinkling of the silver bells that adorned the robes of the Love priestesses.

Citana opened the door wide enough to admit me and my companions. The weeping and jingle of bells drew me past the sitting room into the main bedroom.

Claudia sat on the huge wooden platform bed and held a crying Dragonfly. Claudia wore a plain linen nightshift, her braids cascading down her back. Dragonfly was the first person in Love I saw in formal robes though her public veil had been removed. Her bright yellow tears soaked the shoulder of Claudia's shift.

Dragonfly's second nodded toward the door to the bathing room.

I didn't want to see what had disturbed Dragonfly so, but I forced my boots in that direction. I stopped at the doorway. Gina peered into the room beside me.

A body floated in the pool of jasmine-scented, orange-hot bath water. Equally orange writing marred one of the deep blue marble walls.

"Please tell me the message was written with bath water," I whispered.

Gina swallowed hard. "It's not, m'lady."

In large orange letters, the message read, "You're next, bitch."

Chapter 2

I swallowed hard as well. "Gina, do you recognize who is in the bath?"

"From the bald head, it may be Gregorios," my warden whispered. "I can't really tell with all the blood in the bathwater and the corpse face down. And I can see a stab wound on the back from here. At least the jasmine covers some of the scent of the blood and loose bowels."

My heart sank. Gregorios was Dragonfly's head of household as well as her personal assistant, just as Sivan was mine. They were probably in the process of drawing Dragonfly's bath when they were attacked. However, the stab wound and the message meant this was more than an accidental slip and fall.

"Do you want Dezba and me to remove the corpse from the bath?" Gina asked.

A shiver ran through me. As much as I wanted to believe a current member of the sisterhood or staff within Orrin's Temple of Love had committed this atrocity, I knew better.

"No, the corpse may have a spell on it like Yellow Fin last month," I murmured. The things that had been done to the orphan street urchin were far worse than anything I'd encountered before. However, Gerd's ally Bianca, the former seat of Mother in Orrin, had laid a trap spell on the child's corpse with the intent to kill me and whichever member of Light accompanied me in the investigation. Brother Jeremy's quick thinking and faster action was the only thing that saved us. How close

Bianca's plan came to succeeding made my decision easier. "We wait for assistance."

I strode from the bathing area back to the main door to the high sister's quarters. Sister Shada and Warden Jocasta waited outside in the corridor as I suspected they would. I ordered Shada to send for a Light priest, Master Healer Devin, and High Brother Xander of Death. She didn't question me though technically, I had no authority in her Temple. She trotted down the hallway with Jocasta in tow. With the murder inside their own walls, the wardens would be following their priestesses closer than their own shadows.

I headed back into the sleeping room of Dragonfly's chambers. Twelve help me, I didn't want to interrogate her while she experienced the throes of grief, but I had no choice in the matter.

Dragonfly's weeping had settled to an occasional hiccup when I rounded the chest at the foot of the platform frame and sat next to her on her bed. She pulled herself from Claudia's comforting hold and straightened.

"D-do what you need to do, Anthea." She gulped.

"Not until someone from Light arrives," I said gently as I took her left hand in both of mine. "Right now, I'm here as a friend."

"I-It had to be Gerd." Dragonfly's voice still quavered though her tone grew stronger. The *berda* was number two on my birth mother's list of people she wished dead. Dragonfly had been Gerd's second, and she'd only gone along with Gerd's excesses in an effort to protect the other priestesses at the Temple of Love.

"What makes you say that?" I said.

"No one else could have entered my quarters without Citana or one of the other wardens seeing them."

We both looked at the block of spelled marble guarding the entrance to Orrin's tunnel system. It rested between Dragonfly's vanity table and the first of three wardrobes in the room. My heart tried to climb out of my chest and choke me.

"Chief Justice?" Gina murmured.

I nodded, and my warden dashed out of Dragonfly's chambers. So much had gone wrong in the few months I'd been in my position as Orrin's seat of Balance. So much so, my own wardens knew what I would order next without even the need for silent speech. Gina would gather another warden and check on those guarding the tunnel entrances that lay outside of Orrin's walls while Dezba stayed at my side.

And Dragonfly was correct. Only another member of the clergy could have opened the tunnel entrances. I was damn lucky I'd added extra alarm spells to the tunnel entrance in my own bedchambers. Otherwise, my throat would have been slit as well while I lay sleeping.

"Why weren't you in your bedchambers this morning?" I asked.

"That was my fault," Claudia murmured. "The baby woke me before First Morning."

"He's moving?" I said, trying my best to keep the bitterness from my voice.

Claudia nodded. "It was the first time. I wanted to share it with someone."

"Dragonfly, you're the only sister I've seen in Love in their formal robes." I rubbed her hand. "Why were you still up?"

"Gregorios and I were counting the evening's donations and filling out the ledgers."

Of course, she had been. Gerd's theft from her own Temple was one of her minor crimes. Dragonfly, as the first *berda* to hold a seat in any of the Issuran Temples, had become quite obsessive with following her Temple's procedures.

To the point, where she had a seat from one of the other Temples double-check her counts and sums. Usually, it was me.

She swallowed hard to keep from weeping again. "We had just finished when Ichik fetched me to Claudia's quarters. She worried her assistant unnecessarily." Dragonfly glanced at Claudia and squeezed the other priestess's hand with her right one.

"Wh-when I returned to my quarters, I smelled the bath oils." Dragonfly continued. "I called for Gregorios to assist me with combing out my hair. When he didn't answer, I walked into my bathing room and-and found him." Though she struggled to keep her composure, fresh tears coursed down her cheeks.

I looked up at Citana. "Chief Warden, may I speak to you privately?"

She hesitated for a moment, obviously loath to leave her two priestesses alone after such a horrendous murder had occurred in the next room.

Thankfully, Dezba spoke up. "I swear by the Twelve I'll guard High Sister Dragonfly and Sister Claudia with my life. Just as I know you'll do the same while speaking with Chief Justice Anthea."

Citana nodded curtly. "Very well then."

After a final pat on Dragonfly's hand, I rose from the bed. Citana followed me to the high sister's sitting room and closed the door behind her. She stood at attention, as if she feared I would lash her then and there.

I circled the sitting room, warding it from anyone overhearing our conversation.

"At ease, Chief Warden. I don't blame you for the murder," I said. "I merely wish to establish a timeline."

"Yes, m'lady." She cleared her throat. "However, given the actions of the previous chief warden of Mother, it would be best if you truthspelled me."

"Oh, I will truthspell you, but only when someone from Light arrives." I gestured at one of the cushioned chairs. "For now, can we please speak plainly as civilized adults?"

She nodded more slowly this time. Whatever she expected from me, I wasn't delivering. She sat gingerly on the chair I indicated while I sat across from her.

"What were you doing prior to the high sister retiring to her chambers?"

Her chin lifted. "I was in the worshippers receiving room, guarding the high sister." Citana frowned. "The only odd thing during the evening or night was no one requested personal worship with the high sister."

"Why was this unusual?" I asked.

A rueful smile tilted her mouth. "There's always a handful who believe direct worship with our Temple seat will bring them closer to the Twelve."

"Were activities what you would call normal over the last few days?"

"Yes." This time, Citana chuckled. "I expect a few heat related fights between worshippers. Tempers are often short between the Solstice and the Vintner's Festival."

I cocked my head. "There haven't been any reports of brawling or arrests at your Temple."

She shrugged. "My trainer at the Academy said it's not unusual for rutting behavior to occur at Love. Worshippers sometimes forget they aren't competing for the sisters' attention. A couple of knocks get their attention along with the threat of banning them from the Temple. We learn when it's just stupidity and when there's a real problem with a worshipper."

"Did the Temple end worship at the usual time?"

"Third Evening bells on the last chime," Citana said. "The sisters wind things down with their worshippers before then. It makes my people's job much easier."

"And after the worshippers were cleared from the Temple?" I prompted.

"I escorted the high sister and her assistant to her chambers with the donations box." Citana sagged a bit in her chair. "I stood guard in the corridor for maybe a half candlemark when Ichik approached me, saying Sister Claudia needed the high sister right away."

"Did Ichik enter the high sister's bedchambers with his message?"

"No." Citana shook her head vigorously. "I made them wait in the corridor. Both I and my wardens have been following the guidelines the chief wardens devised after the assassination attempts on the seats this spring."

"That's good," I murmured. "I take it you relayed the message?"

Citana nodded. "When I entered this room, the high sister was at her desk." The chief warden gestured toward the corner where a familiar ledger rested on a small, ornate maple desk. Dragonfly's workspace was always far neater than my own.

"I gave the high sister the message," Citana continued. "Then I escorted her to Sister Claudia's quarters."

"What about Gregorios?" I asked.

"I-I left them alone," Citana choked out. "Th-they weren't even here when Gerd was Love's seat. I've heard stories about her, but there was no reason . . ."

"Gregorios earned Dragonfly's affection and respect," I said. "In her twisted mind, that would be enough for Gerd. She couldn't kill Dragonfly through the happenstance of Claudia's son making his presence known. Therefore, the way to hurt Dragonfly would be to harm someone she cared about."

"Logically, I know your words are true, Chief Justice." A wan smile appeared on Citana's face. "However, I trusted in magic too much to guard that one egress, and I allowed my high priestess's wish for privacy to circumvent my better judgment. Both Little Bear and Sabine are right. It's better to wound your seat's pride than to find them dead."

I blinked at her mention of mine and Thief's chief wardens. It explained Little Bear's grumbling about Luc refusing to use the front door when High Brother Xander did so in his visits with Yanaba. And Talbert's chief warden had someone stationed in his bedchambers for months before the assassination attempts on me last winter.

Even when Talbert was elsewhere performing his duties.

No wonder Citana was cross with herself. If not for Claudia and Luc's son, Dragonfly would have been the one floating face down in her bath.

"Were you the one who discovered the body, or was it Dragonfly?" I murmured.

"Dragonfly entered through the main door." Citana gestured at the entrance to the high sister's chambers. "I heard her scream, and I rushed in. She was kneeling at the entrance to her bath. A few moments later, Sister Claudia, Ichik, and Warden Jocasta entered the bedchamber as I tried to pull the high sister away from the sight. Warden Jocasta said she heard the high sister cry out in her mind. She has a passive talent for silent speech."

Citana took a shuddering breath before she continued. "Sister Claudia and Warden Jocasta assisted me in moving the high sister to her bed. Then Sister Claudia ordered Ichik to fetch you." The chief warden's face heated at the last confession. It was probably mere embarrassment that Love's second kept her composure and had the wherewithal to summon me after the discovery of the crime.

"Thank you, Chief Warden," I said. "I will have to truthspell you later, but thank you for helping me now."

"I understand, m'lady." A ghost of a smile flitted across her face. "And you're welcome."

There was a knock on the main door, and we both rose. I lowered my wards, and Chief Warden Citana crossed the room to answer the door. I automatically drew one of my daggers. When Citana opened the door, relief spread through me at the sight of High Brother Luc of Light and his chief warden Nicholas.

"Really, Chief Justice? Can't I get through First Morning worship services once before you summon me?" Luc teased as he swung into Dragonfly's bedchamber on his crutches. The little twinge of guilt I constantly felt over the loss of his left foot hit harder than usual. Especially since Gerd was ultimately responsible for his torture.

I shoved my guilt back into its hole. "It's much worse than that," I answered. "I haven't had my morning tea, much less broken my fast yet."

My dark sense of humor couldn't hold up under the emotional strain. I looked at the door to Dragonfly's bedroom and back at Luc. "We believe its the high sister's personal assistant. I didn't allow the wardens to touch the corpse in the bath, yet."

"Dragonfly?" Luc cocked his head, a shocked expression on his handsome features.

"We'll have to truthspell her to confirm it, but hers and Chief Warden Citana's preliminary testimony says no," I murmured.

Nicholas's attention shifted to Citana. "How could anyone enter a seat's quarters—"

But Luc's countenance hardened, and his skin shifted to a deep red. "Gerd."

"Gina is checking on the guards at each of the exits of the tunnel system," I said.

Luc drew in a deep breath and released it. "Thank you for waiting for one of Light to arrive."

I shrugged. "After the incident with Yellow Fin, I learned my lesson."

Ironically, Luc's second Jeremy *had* been with me that time. I discovered just how far my opponents would go after conventional assassination attempts against me repeatedly failed. It was a depth that chilled me to my core.

Luc looked at Nicholas. "No one enters or leaves High Sister Dragonfly's chambers without mine or the chief justice's permission.

"Understood, High Brother." Nicholas's thick blue moustache and beard wiggled with his acknowledgement. I never understood why so many men of Toscan and Briton descent bothered with facial hair when they kept the rest of the hair on their head so short.

I pivoted and headed back into the main bedchamber, Luc and Citana on my heels. Dragonfly inclined her head to Luc, but it was Claudia's sweet smile in his direction that set my teeth on edge. I tried to shove my jealousy into the same hole as my guilt but I was running out of room to store my emotions.

However, Dezba appeared very relieved at my return. No doubt Dragonfly's grief made the reserved young warden uncomfortable.

"High Sister, Sister, could you please wait in the sitting room while we . . . deal with things in here?" I said.

"Of course," Claudia murmured. Dragonfly merely nodded.

Once they were out of the room, Luc said silently, *We should take Dragonfly to Mya.*

I was thinking the same thing. After everything the sisters of Love had been through, High Sister Mya and the rest of the clergy of Child had more work ahead dealing with additional emotional damage to priestesses and staff of this Temple.

"Shall we pull the corpse out of the high sister's bath?" Luc asked. "Or do you wish to do the rewind first?"

"The rewind."

I examined the two rooms again, trying to calculate the best way to conduct a rewind. My own sisterhood needed three dimensions to anchor our senses while we manipulated the fourth dimension, time. The problem was a rewind acted the same way as a ward. It used the wall as a base and covered any windows or doors. I propped my right elbow on my opposing forearm and tapped my right forefinger against my lips as I consider the problem.

"How hard would it be to remove the bathing room door?" I asked.

The two wardens looked at each other in confusion before Citana said, "We would need a claw hammer to pry out the hinge pins."

"You wouldn't happen to have one available in Love, would you?" I asked.

"I'll have to check with our maintenance person, m'lady."

"Please do so."

Once she left the bedroom to fetch the tool, Luc frowned. "What the demon are you trying to do?"

"If we're right and Gerd is behind the murder, both the bathing room and the bedchamber would be involved," I said.

"And what?" Luc stared at as if he were questioning whether I needed care from the Temple of Child as well. "You're too lazy to perform two rewinds?"

A little hiccupping sound came from Dezba.

"Don't stab him for the insult just yet, Warden," I teased. "I'm not sure if my idea will work."

"But you did a rewind for several blocks during the investigation of Old Anne's murder," Dezba said. "This is only two rooms."

"I also used Justice Yanaba and her bond with Orrin itself as the anchor for that spell," I said. "This rewind needs to be fine-tuned, and I'm not risking her or her baby. I shouldn't have done it the last time."

"What exactly are you planning, Anthea?" From Luc's expression, he'd made up his mind that I was mad after all.

"We take off the door, and in essence, make the two rooms as one." I gestured at the open doorway to the bathing room. "I'll position myself on the sill. One of you will be in the bathing room to witness, and the other out here in the bedchamber."

"I don't remember you ever trying anything like this before," Luc said. "Are you sure it will work?"

"No." I grinned at him. "But then, I wasn't sure the stunt with Yanaba and the four city blocks would work either. If it doesn't, then yes, I'll have to break down the rewinds, but if this works we'll have a solid chain of events in the high sister's quarters."

Chief Warden Citana returned with a claw hammer in her hand. "Bless her heart. Our maintenance person Iona had one. I was worried I would have to borrow one from the Smiths Guild."

We all chuckled. The Smiths Guild wasn't known for their sharing, plus I'd made them look like selfish fools at the last city meeting. If Citana had to go to any smith and they'd known I was the one who requested the claw hammer, there would have been a hefty price to pay, someway, somehow.

Luc and I stayed out of the two wardens' way as they made quick work of the pins and carefully propped the huge slab of heavily lacquered and sealed wood against the closest wardrobe.

"Are you sure about this, Anthea?" he asked.

"No."

"But you're going to do it anyway?" Luc looked at me askance.

I merely returned his gaze.

He made an exasperated sound. "Some day, I'll learn not to ask ridiculous questions."

Citana leaned close to Dezba. "Is this normal investigative behavior?"

"For them? Yes." The corners of Dezba's mouth quirked as she looked at Luc and me.

"You are all mad." Citana shook her head.

"Oh, definitely," Luc grumbled.

"Who made you the high brother of Child?" I said.

He ignored me and swung forward on his crutches. "I'll take the bathing room, Warden."

"But, High Brother." Dezba took a step toward him. "I don't want you to slip and fall into the bathing pool."

Luc's irritation spiked through my mind, and I had to bite the inside of my lower lip to keep from laughing aloud. He slowly pivoted to face Dezba. Her skin grew a brilliant red shade as she realized she'd overstepped propriety.

"My dear, Warden Dezba." His smile wasn't his usual charming one. "I am beginning to understand why the chief justice finds the entire Balance corps of wardens particularly vexing at times." He twisted back toward his destination and stomped into the bathing room.

"Ignore him," I said to Dezba. "He hasn't broken his fast either, and you know how testy I am without tea and that first meal of the day."

"Yes, m'lady." She bobbed her head.

On the other hand, Citana appeared as if she were about to call for reinforcements.

I gestured for the women to back away from the tunnel entrance. "Chief Warden, if you would stand with Warden Dezba, we can get started."

Dezba led Citana to the corner between Dragonfly's bed and the door to her sitting room, the farthest they could be away from me and still observe everything. That didn't account for the nervous ripples coming off Citana's psyche.

"Chief Warden, have you ever observed a rewind spell?" I asked.

"Only during class at the academy, m'lady," she murmured. "Even something as minor of seeing myself from the day before was unsettling."

"Think of it as watching an athletic competition in a square on a field," Dezba reassured the older woman. "I will report what I see to the chief justice. However, if you notice anything odd or unusual, please speak."

Citana nodded.

Satisfied the chief warden understood, I folded back the rugs closest to the bathing room and exposed the bare marble before I settled myself on the sill. Thankfully, this would be a fairly short rewind. I didn't think my buttocks could deal with straddling the narrow length of marble if I were pulling the timelines past First Night.

I ignored the hard edges digging into my thighs and calves, placed my palms on the slabs of floor marble on each side of the sill, and took a deep breath to still my mind. Whispering the words of the spell, I reached out and yanked the past toward me.

On this occasion, no trap spell or anything else came flying along the time lines to attack me. I pulled until First Night and let the time lines flow forward a little faster than normal between my fingers.

For a few moments, Luc and Dezba alternately called out, "Nothing." Finally, Dezba shouted, "Slower."

I gritted my teeth and slowed the velocity.

"Chief Warden Citana enters the room with an oil lamp," Dezba recited. "She checks beneath the bed, opens the wardrobes, and enters the bathing room."

Luc picked up the recitation, but his voice echoed oddly with the marble and water. "Citana enters and lights the lamp in the corner of the bathing room across from the door. She looks around. She seems satisfied no one is here and leaves."

Dezba picked up the events. "The chief warden passes through the bedchamber again. She places the lamp she carries on the stand next to the high sister's bed, and she exits."

I almost let the time lines speed up, but Dezba said, "High Sister Dragonfly enters her bedchamber. She heads straight for the bathing chamber."

"Dragonfly walks in, and—really, Anthea? Must I tell you this?" Luc complained.

"Yes," I hissed.

"The high sister relieves herself in a chamber pot and leaves," Luc growled.

"The high sister passes through the bedchamber and goes to the sitting room," Dezba said.

I let the time lines slip a little faster through my fingers. So far, the only thing Dragonfly left out of her statement earlier was her pause to take care of her personal needs.

Once again, Dezba shouted, "Slower!"

Perspiration that had nothing to do with the summer heat trickled down my back as my fingers tightened around the time lines.

"The stone guarding the passage to the tunnel system folds back," Dezba said. "A cloaked and hooded figure enters the bedchamber. I cannot see their face. They glance in the direction of the bed before closing the tunnel entrance. They turn toward the bath chamber and cross the room."

Footsteps came toward me. Deep down, I knew it was Dezba attempting to see the face of the assassin, but I couldn't help raising my head.

A ghostly image of my birth mother Gerd stared down at me, and she had a knife in her hand.

Chapter 3

Despite my suspicions, the reality unnerved me. The shock nearly made me release the time lines, but I squeezed my fingers tightly. The faint form of Gerd froze in place. Thankfully, neither Luc or Dezba said a word while I gathered my composure.

Or what little was left of it.

I swallowed my heart and let the events unfold. However, I winced as the memory of Gerd passed through me.

"It's Gerd," Luc said, his voice bitter. "She is armed, and she positions herself behind the bathing room door."

The very same door I had the two wardens remove.

"Gregorios is coming into the bedchamber through the sitting room door," Dezba said. She was still on this side of Dragonfly's sleeping quarters. "They pause to lay out sleepwear and collect towels from the second wardrobe. Now, they enter the bathing room."

Once again, Luc picked up the recitation. "They enter the bathing room. They stop the drain and turn on the spigot to fill the pool. Gregorios selects oils from the shelves in here, kneels by the pool, and adds them to the bath. They stand and return the bottles. They reach down to turn off the spigot. Gerd slips from behind the door and raises her arm holding the knife. Gregorios is unaware of her presence. They start to rise. She stabs Gregorios in the back."

Luc's fury at watching Gerd destroy someone else beat against my psyche. My fingers and lungs burned while I tried to maintain control of the spell.

"Discipline your emotions, High Brother." I spat the words as if they were a poison I attempted to expel before it killed me. His rage receded enough I could breathe again.

"Gregorios starts to topple into the pool," Luc said. "But she wrenches out the blade, grabs their ear, and slits their throat. Gerd manages to knock them over to the far side of the room."

Luc's crutches thump against the marble and his voice hardens as he forces himself to continue witnessing. "The blood collects on the marble tiles. Gerd wipes her knife on Gregorios's trousers and sheathes it. She dips her right fingers into the blood and starts writing on the wall. Gregorios is trying to get up. She stomps on his left temple with her boot heel. They are lying on the floor, no longer moving."

He tried to contain his rage, but it bubbled up again. I didn't have the heart to say anything. Not when he was reliving his own pain as well as Gregorios's.

"She finishes writing the message," Luc continued. "She washes her hands in the pool and dries them on Gregorios's tunic before she shoves him into the water. She walks out of the bathing room."

"Gerd comes into the bedroom," Dezba continued. "She stares at the high sister's bed. She partially draws her knife." There's a long pause in her recitation. "After six breaths, she rams her knife back into the sheath. She sharply turns to the tunnel entrance. The stone folds open, and she slips through the exit. The stone folds back into place."

We were close to the end of the rewind. I let the threads of time speed just a bit through my fingers.

"The high sister enters her bedchamber again," Dezba said. "She removes her veil and calls out. She cocks her head as if waiting for an answer. She calls out again before she strides towards the bathing room."

I couldn't breathe. Shock and grief rip through me at the sight in the pool, but I'm seeing the body in red clothing floating in red water through someone else's eyes. Someone with normal vision, not my odd sight. I started screaming. And time snapped back into place.

Chapter 4

Luc held a cup of wine to my lips. I couldn't stop my hands from trembling to take the cup from him. We were back in Dragonfly's sitting room. Luc sat on one side of me. Dragonfly fretted on the other.

I drank a few sips of the wine before I said, "Wh-what happened?"

"There was enough psychic residue—" he started.

"I'm so sorry, Anthea." Dragonfly grabbed my left hand.

"You were in shock when you found Gregorios." I squeezed her hand back. "Not your fault. I've never had something like that happen during a rewind."

"You usually aren't sitting right on top of the spot where someone was murdered or discovered the corpse," Luc bit out. "Nor have you tried two enclosed places at once."

"Could you please restrain your annoyance with me?" I massaged my temples. The pain seemed like a solid rod had been inserted through them with a detour into my eyeballs. "My head already aches, and your leaking emotions are not helping."

"That rewind was not worth your life," Dragonfly snapped at me.

"You are not helping the pain either," I muttered.

"And the rewind was necessary to confirm Gerd was the culprit behind Gregorios's murder," Chief Warden Citana said.

"She wanted us to know," I said. "Specifically, she wanted to make sure I knew." I stood and took one step before my balance wavered. Dezba jumped to my side and steadied me before I toppled to the carpets. I pretended I didn't almost fall and said, "Luc, let's double-check Gregorios before we haul him out of Dragonfly's bath, but I have a feeling there's no trap spell on his corpse."

"You should rest, Anthea." Dragonfly rose to her full height. The *berda* was a good head taller than me, and I was tall for a woman.

"If you seek to intimidate me by towering over me—" I started.

"Enough, you two!" Claudia's bells jangled as she laboriously climbed to her feet. She had gone to her chambers to dress before coming back to Dragonfly's quarters. While she had not bothered with her public veil, the bells on her robes chimed discordantly with her vexation at us. "We have enough problems without sniping at each other."

Luc stood as well. "She's right. Gerd wanted to prove she could get to any of us. She could just as easily have slit Dragonfly's throat if she'd been in bed instead of attending to Claudia. I'm surprised she didn't slash mine or Anthea's this morning."

A wave of dizziness swept through me that had nothing to do with my empathetic reaction to Dragonfly's emotion or my fear of my birth mother's next tactic, and everything to do with the wine in my empty stomach.

"Anthea?" Concern flowed from Luc.

"I'm fine." I shot him a smile. "It has more to do with unwatered wine before breaking my fast."

"Then I'll fetch you some unleavened bread and milk with a bit of honey," Claudia declared. "It did wonders for my morning sickness." She left the sitting room with Warden Jocasta on her heels.

"I really wish she wouldn't do that," I murmured.

"What?" Dragonfly cocked her head. "Be kind to you?"

"Yes." I sighed. "It makes me feel guilty."

Luc said nothing, and I immediately regretted my words. The edict wasn't his or Claudia's fault. I simply didn't know how to deal with my anger and frustration over the whole situation. Maybe I was the one who needed to seek High Sister Mya's care after all.

As I suspected, there was no additional spell on the dead person in the bathing room. If Gerd wanted me dead, that would have been the fastest, smartest way to kill me.

Unless she knew about Bianca's attempt a few weeks ago.

High Brother Xander of Death and Master Healer Devin arrived a few moments after Dezba and I fished the corpse from Dragonfly's bath with Chief Warden Nicholas's aid. Even I could discern the body was Gregorios.

Devin crouched on the tiles next to the dead man. "Are you sure you want a full examination of the corpse, Chief Justice? The wounds match your rewind."

"I don't want to leave anything to chance, Master Devin," I said. "Not when it comes to Gerd."

The healer looked up at Xander standing next to him. "Do you concur, High Brother?"

The poor priest was barely four years older than my junior justice Yanaba. He didn't deserve the weight of the strife between the Temple of Death and the Healers Guild on his young shoulders. Luckily, he'd learned quite a bit from Bertrice prior to her passing, including the dance between the two factions. I often found I needed both sides' assistance in learning the truth of a case.

"I have a few more years experience with my former high sister than you do, Master Devin." A wry smile tilted Xander's mouth. "Therefore, I concur with the chief justice. We all need to be thorough in our duties. The fact Gerd has resorted to active violence bothers me more than I care to admit."

"She was rather active in her previous murder attempts," I pointed out. "Especially Sister Gretchen's."

"Prior to Gregorios, she manipulated other people to perform her unethical or illegal actions," Xander said. "For example, hiring the Assassins Guild to stab you on the steps of Light or bespelling Magistrate DiCook to bear false witness against you during the winter convocation." Xander shook his head. "I would suggest consulting with Child, but the change in Gerd's behavior means some other factor has shifted. People simply don't alter their demeanor randomly. Any information at this point would assist us in finding her."

"Us?"

"Since the renegades and the Assassins Guild appear to have some sort of alliance with the demons and skinwalkers, then every member of the Twelve Temples is threatened." He frowned. "Including myself and my children."

Did that mean he and Yanaba were going to continue their relationship after the birth of their current babe? The home Temples hadn't put an end date on the breeding edict.

I looked at Luc, guilt weighing on my heart. "What say you, High Brother?"

"I would agree with our brother of Death." He glanced at the corpse before looking at me again. "Honestly, I wondered if Gerd had dumped poison in the bath water. I worried I had missed something during the rewind. I feared for you and the wardens when you pulled Gregorios from the bath water." He shook his head. "I don't know if any of us at Light will be of use to you, except maybe Garbhan."

Now, what had happened among the members of Light that he would say such a thing in front of a peer from another Temple?

Chapter 5

Gina returned from her errand while I nibbled on the unleavened bread and sipped the sweetened milk in Dragonfly's sitting room. High Brother Jax of Wildling and High Brother Talbert of Thief accompanied her. Both priests' expressions were as grim as Gina's.

Luc groaned. "How many did we lose?"

"The two wardens and the pair of peacekeepers at the Duke's entrance," Gina reported. "I've informed the magistrate, who in turn will inform Duke Marco. Magistrate DiCook has requested a meeting as soon as you are done with High Brother Xander and the Healers Guild."

"Damn, we are too predictable," I muttered.

"Sister Farrah and Sister Cedar Grove along with our chief wardens are leading the search for Gerd," Jax said.

"High Brother Han and the magistrate are doubling the guards at all the exits," Talbert added.

"How did Gerd overcome all four guards?" Xander asked.

"Demon magick," Jax spat.

The unleavened bread and milk churned in my stomach. For a moment, I feared I would ruin Dragonfly's carpets. She began rubbing my back while I struggled to get my emotions in check. Now, I understood Luc's odd comment. I was too close to this situation. I wasn't thinking clearly. Yet, I was the perfect bait.

"She planned to use that demon grimoire herself." I looked at Luc.

His skin turned a brilliant pink. He began cursing. In Issuran. In Cantan. Even a few words of Diné and Comanche we'd learned during the siege of Tandor.

Once he ran out of breath, Talbert asked, "Hasn't the grimoire been destroyed?"

I inhaled to answer and paused. The Reverend Mother and Yanaba said it had been destroyed, but what if it hadn't been? What if someone pulled the same trick I had by substituting a demon-contaminated tome?

"The home Temple reported it was, but I don't know for sure," I admitted.

This time, Dragonfly cursed fluently in several languages, including a few I didn't recognize. She finished with, "Has your Reverend Mother become completely daft in her old age!"

I described my actions to fool the renegades who had abducted Luc last winter. "It's entirely possible the Reverend Mother thought she had destroyed the real grimoire."

Talbert rubbed his chin as he considered my words. "And whoever made the exchange would still be at the home Temple to aid Gerd in her escape." He shook his head. "This doesn't bode well at all."

"In other words, I need to call a convocation," I muttered. "I really miss being on a circuit. Being a city seat has become a pain in my buttocks."

No one laughed at my sarcastic comment. Not even Luc.

Technically, I had broken my fast at Love with the unleavened bread and sweetened milk. It did eventually settle my stomach as Claudia had promised. However, it wasn't the heartier meal Deborah, my cook at Balance, usually served me. My stomach growled obnoxiously through the healers' examination of Gregorios's corpse.

To the point, Master Healer Bly asked if I needed something to settle my digestive system.

The healers' examination of Gregorios's body provided no more information. It merely showed Gerd's knife penetrated the head of household's lung. The pain and inability to take a full breath stunned Gregorios, allowing Gerd to slit his throat which was the killing strike. And then there was the cracked skull where she stomped on Gregorios's head. Their murder was so simple, so straight forward.

And so unlike Gerd's normal style.

Which was exactly what Magistrate DiCook said when we met at the Temple of Light.

By then, it was First Afternoon. Thank the Twelve, Luc had inherited High Brother Kam's chef. The man had adapted to Luc's simpler tastes instead of producing the delicacies my maternal grandfather preferred. But Light's chef still had a way with herbs and spices that made even a simple soup taste like a meal fit for the Twelve Themselves.

The magistrate wasn't one to turn down an offer of hospitality from either Light or Balance. DiCook feared offending his wife by honestly telling her how bad her kitchen skills were, but as Deborah, pointed out on more than one occasion, Madame DiCook's talents would not improve if he wasn't truthful.

Once our clergy, chief wardens, and the magistrate gathered in the high brother's dining room and food had been served, Brother Jeremy rose and cast wards so we could have a private conversation.

DiCook turned to me as Jeremy resumed his seat. "Speaking of wardens, why on earth are you putting so much responsibility on Warden Gina's shoulders? She should have a promotion for all the extra work she's doing."

"She's been offered a chief warden position. Three times." I held up the requisite number of fingers. "She turned down Dragonfly. Yanaba and Elizabeth both believe if they stay at my Temple long enough, they will seduced Gina into accepting an offer when they are assigned a seat."

"The queen isn't thinking of rebuilding Tandor, is she?" DiCook looked aghast.

"She can't," Luc said around a mouthful of yeast roll and butter. "Not without killing anyone who steps inside the walls." He swallowed his mouthful of bread. "According to the ancient histories, Death's final defense spells render a space uninhabitable for a thousand generations."

"And?" DiCook prompted.

"Your ancestors were from the isles of Britannia." Luc shrugged. "If you want to put the spells to the test, be my guest."

"The last word from the Reverend Mother said the queen is considering moving the citizens of Tandor to the Anacapa Islands," Elizabeth said before DiCook could spit out an impolite rejoinder at Luc. "If she does, Yanaba and I will be assigned there, and a new junior justice will be assigned to Orrin."

"Won't they be subject to pirate attacks?" Luc's chief warden Nicholas asked.

"Not if Duchess Nadine succeeds in her efforts to build solid fortresses on all the islands," Jeremy said. "The islands would then become her new duchy. She's already approached several foreign ambassadors about trade agreements. If they stop at one of the island wharves, it would lessen their travel a half day each way."

I sipped my wine to keep from laughing. There was no doubt he'd gotten that information through Sister Shi Hua from the way her skin shifted from orange to red.

Brother Garbhan, Luc's newest priest at Light, whistled. "Does Duke Marco know about this?"

"Yes, he does." I set my goblet down. "Lady Alessa has been assisting Duchess Nadine with his blessing."

"And acting as a chaperone for the poor widow?" DiCook raised his right eyebrow.

I snorted. "Some of Marco's idiot cousins foolishly think the duchess has more than her title. I don't blame her for wanting a bodyguard."

"And we are deliberately avoiding the real subject of this meeting." Yanaba unerringly spooned the mixture of berries, milk, and sweet bread from her bowl to her mouth. The poor justice was keeping down food now, but only certain things. She avoided most of the Cantan dishes Luc's chef prepared, but he always made her something special that wouldn't upset her delicate stomach.

"You all know Gerd, the former high sister of Love, entered the Temple in the predawn hour and murdered Love's head of household Gregorios," Luc began.

"Are we sure it was Gerd?" Yanaba asked.

Elizabeth frowned. "Are you saying Anthea performed the rewind incorrectly?"

"No." Yanaba set her spoon in her bowl. "A rewind only allows us to replay events as they happened within that space. What if it were a skinwalker or a demon wearing Gerd? It would explain her unusual behavior."

Luc and I exchanged looks. We were both slipping in objectiveness.

"Or Gerd's change in behavior could be the result of having nothing to lose," Nicholas murmured. "She has a death sentence over her head regardless of what she does now."

"Yanaba may be right." I pushed my plate back, no longer having an appetite for the fresh roasted fish. "Demon magic was used to kill the guards at the Duke's entrance to the tunnel system."

"Maybe it would be best to bring down the three remaining exits," Little Bear said. "This isn't the first time the damn renegades and demons have used them against us."

"We've already doubled the people watching the tunnels, including adding a member of the clergy at each of them," DiCook protested. "If Gerd tries again—"

"Do you really want to sacrifice more of your peacekeepers, Malven?"

I said. "If Yanaba is right, the demon or skinwalker is using those guards' death to power itself. If I'm right and it is really Gerd, she's no longer a priestess. She has been studying the demon grimoire formerly in her possession, or she's found another one. No matter which is the case, she's in the process of becoming a skinwalker herself by casting demon spells."

Red drained from DiCook's face, leaving it an ugly yellow color. "What are you saying? Gerd is fated to destroy Orrin no matter what we do?"

"No," Luc said firmly. "I'm betting the person who entered Love is definitely Gerd. Otherwise, a demon would have targeted Balance and Death first, especially after those Temples managed to destroy an entire demon army in Tandor."

"What happens if Jax and Talbert's people lose the trail?" Shi Hua said softly. Like me, she'd pushed back her plate with the food barely touched. "Or worse, the murder at Love was bait for a trap? The renegades led us on a merry little trip when they abducted you, High Brother."

Luc stared across the table at me. His worry prickled against my psyche.

I shrugged. "High Brother Xander is right. I'll call for an emergency convocation for tonight on what to do about the tunnels and finding Gerd."

Chapter 6

Thankfully, the message regarding tonight's emergency convocation went out before Lady Katarina's unplanned and unannounced arrival at the Temple of Balance. Her visit resulted in no work being done because every single priestess, warden, and staff member, including our underage squires, doted over Lord Kam.

Well, except me and the three wardens on guard duty. Unfortunately, I didn't have the excuse of watching the Temple walls and entrances. Therefore, while everyone else ooo'd and ahh'd over the infant noble, Katarina dragged me to my office with the words, "We must talk."

The last thing I needed right now was some idiotic problem with the nobility.

"What in the world is going on?" I asked. When she took a seat on one of the visitor's chairs, I circled my desk and dropped into my own chair. "Is there an issue with Duchess Nadine?"

"Don't play coy with me, Anthea." Katarina leaned forward, a scowl accenting her bright pink visage. "I heard through the fishwives Gerd was seen in Orrin."

So much for keeping that news quiet. If Katarina knew, then everyone else in Orrin had already heard about the incident at Love. Duke Marco was adamant about keeping his wife in the dark so as not to upset her when her focus should be on their child.

However, Katarina and I shared an odd bond. Both of our mothers were priestesses of Love, and we were both products of the Spring Rituals. Which was why when she suspected her husband was in one of his protective moods, she came straight to me. I simply didn't have the heart to lie to her.

I groaned and sagged in my chair. "Tell me what you already know so I'm not repeating myself."

Katarina repeated enough of a chunk of what happened at Love this morning that I suspected it was one of the sisters who'd passed the information. The question of whether it was directly or through pillow talk with Lady Alessa didn't matter. But what the duke's wife added to her tale aroused my interest.

"Do you know Alo, the innkeeper of the Green Lady?" Katarina asked.

"We've met a couple of times since I was assigned to Orrin." That was an understatement of the generation. I'd used the entrance to the tunnel system inside his establishment a few times myself to avoid the spies watching me since I became chief justice of Orrin.

"His daughter Chumana claims she saw a woman matching Gerd's description try to access the tunnel system," Katarina stated.

"And who is the source for this tale?" I said, my skepticism more than evident.

"Chumana herself." Katarina slapped the surface of my desk with her palm. "I spoke with her during the midday meal not a half candlemark ago.

I cocked my head and grinned. "Marco let you off the ducal estate?"

"My old master at the Veterinarians Guild sent a message asking for assistance healing a cow herd suffering from udder infections." She shrugged. "My dear husband could not deny assistance to one of his people."

"Not without causing more hurt feelings." I laughed at the fight I was sure the noble couple had before Katarina probably threatened his manhood. "I'm glad you're using your healing skills for the good of our cattle population."

"You'll be glad when you're plowing through a steak at my dining table." She smiled briefly at her rejoinder before her visage turned grim once again. "Seriously though, Anthea. You do need to question Chumana under a truthspell. She may be able to give you more details. Something that will lead you to Gerd. She's destroyed enough lives in Orrin."

"A question for you first, m'lady." I leaned forward and rested my elbows on my desk. "Why were you at the Green Lady?"

"I used to take an occasional meal there with my mother," she said wistfully. "Mother would disguise herself as a man, just to get away from the Temple once in a while. I was feeling a bit nostalgic after helping my old guild master."

My heart sank. For Katarina's mother to sneak away for a little peace and quiet said how truly bad things were underneath Gerd's management. That was long before the demons came to Orrin. And I could understand Katarina wanting to relive one of her few happy memories.

"Very well then." I nodded. "Thank you for the information. I will follow up on it."

"Don't placate me, Chief Justice," Katarina said as she rose. "I grew up at Love. Gerd's intent was to kill High Sister Dragonfly this morning. If she finds a way into Balance, she'll slit your throat and enjoy every drop of blood draining from your body."

"I'm not placating you, m'lady." I pushed to my feet. "And I'm under no illusion she would kill me immediately. She'll torture me because she can no longer do so to her parents, and she blames us all for her misfortunes."

Katarina made an unladylike snort. "She had everything a person could possibly want. Wealth, power, status. None of it was enough, and that lies solely on her. Not you. Not your grandparents."

I shook my head. "The problem is she doesn't care how many people get in her way on her quest for retribution."

And I'd already almost lost Luc, Sivan, and Nathan in Gerd's attempts on my life. Even worse, I'd lost former High Brother Kam of Light, my grandfather, to her schemes. I'll be damned to the demon realm if I let anything like that happen again.

Chapter 7

I wasn't in the best of moods when Little Bear, Shi Hua, Mateqai, and I rode across the city. Whispers and murmurs followed in our wake. I hadn't been wrong in my guess that the entire city knew about this morning's murder at Love.

Luc hadn't been happy about my request for Shi Hua's assistance either. However, the pregnant sister from Jing would be less scary to a child.

Even a child who lived up to the name meaning "snake maiden" in my encounters with her.

A few early diners sat in the inn when we entered the establishment. All of them peered our way with open curiosity. Alo approached us, his hands held out in invitation.

"Chief Justice, Sister, Wardens! How may I serve you? Our specialty this evening is roasted ahi. Fresh caught!" Alo paused to take a breath. He was an average-sized man. He wore an apron over the loose cotton shirts and pants of his Cliffdweller ancestors, along with straight bangs and the rest of his hair pulled into a neat bun on the back of his head.

I inclined my head at his enthusiastic greeting. "Actually, we need to speak to your daughter, Chumana, my dear innkeeper."

His demeanor immediately shifted to fear. "Has my daughter been accused of a crime?"

"No, Alo," I said softly. "However, she may be a witness."

He lowered his voice as well. "This morning's murder?"

I groaned again at the evidence of the efficiency of the city's fishwives. "So everyone in Orrin knows about it?"

He gestured in the general direction of the Temples. "Anything to do with you, m'lady, is of great interest to all the citizens of the duchy. Let me get Chumana. I'm assuming you need privacy for speaking with her?"

I nodded. He pivoted and headed toward the kitchen of the inn. A moment later, he exited with Chumana in tow. Both of them carried multiple tankards.

"This way, Chief Justice!" His enthusiasm returned, or else, he tried to hide both his fear and that Chumana was involved in this morning's incident.

Somehow.

He ushered us into a small private dining room. Its fireplace was as cold as the one in the main dining area, thank the Twelve. The heat of this summer meant only cook fires burned. In turn, the muscles around my eyes didn't ache from my continuous squinting.

Chumana set the two tankards she carried on the table and curtsied before me. "Father said you wished to speak with me, Lady Justice. How may I serve?"

She was far more polite than she had been the first time I entered the Green Lady, but then, I had been disguised as a man using the tunnels to seek solace at Love. Still, there was an edge to her voice I recognized as fear.

"You're not in trouble, Chumana." I pushed back my hood and smiled at her. She did not appear reassured, but then, my red eyes discomforted most humans. "Please sit down. I need to ask you some questions about a person who came to your father's inn."

She frowned and looked up at Alo before looking back at me. "Surely, Father could answer your questions better than me about anyone who has entered the Green Lady."

"Perhaps." I pulled one of the chairs from the table and settled on it. "But you may have the information I need."

"I don't know nothing." The girl's voice rose in panic.

"Are you calling the duke's wife a liar?" I asked firmly.

The girl's eyes widened, and she looked up at Alo. "I swear I was entertaining the lady like you asked!"

"Hush, Chumana." He wrapped an arm around his daughter and hugged her. "Let the chief justice ask her questions."

The girl gulped and faced me again. "W-will you have to truthspell me? Will I die?"

"Well, actually that's the reason I brought Sister Shi Hua with me." I gestured toward the Light priestess. "She's far more gentle with a truthspell than I am. And it will only hurt if you try to lie in answer to my questions."

After a moment, Chumana reluctantly nodded. She pulled out the chair and plunked her slight body down upon the wooden seat. Shi Hua followed suit with the chair across the table from me.

"May I stay while you question my daughter?" Alo murmured.

"Yes, but I ask that you do not repeat anything that is said within these walls." I scowled at him. "For your sakes as well as the rest of your family's, not just ours."

Alo nodded.

Chief Justice, you might want to ward the room first, Shi Hua said silently. *There's a scullery maid outside of the door, attempting to listen in.*

I threw my senses in that direction, and sure enough, a woman was busy making it look like she was cleaning the closest tables and benches in the main dining area. It was probably the cleanest anything in an entire inn had ever been.

Demons take them all. These days, I could never be sure if someone spying on me was an enemy or someone who wanted the status of being the first to know the latest gossip. At least, Lady Katarina had brought her news straight to me instead of sharing it with all the nobles in the duchy.

I rose and quickly warded the room. Alo shot nervous looks at Little Bear and Mateqai before he sat in the chair across from Chumana. I resumed my seat and nodded to Shi Hua. Light magic tingled across my skin as the priestess laid the truth spell on the girl.

"Listen carefully, Chumana," I murmured. "You are not in trouble. Lady Katarina said she spoke with you when she stopped here for the midday meal. She believes you may have some information regarding someone who committed a crime without realizing you know this information. I will ask you a series of questions. As long as you tell me the truth to the best of your ability, the truthspell won't hurt you. If you don't know the answer to the question, simply say, 'I don't know'. Do you understand?"

She nodded.

I chuckled. "Chumana, for future reference, if another justice speaks with you, you will need to say the words. My sisters cannot see you nod your head."

"Oh! I'm so sorry, Lady Justice!" She glanced at her father, who gave her an encouraging wave of his hand. "Yes, m'lady. I understand your instructions."

"Thank you. What is your name?" I said.

"Chumana." The girl looked at me as if I were mad. Of course, this would be her first experience with a formal questioning.

"What is your father's name?"

"Alo." Her brows drew together in confusion.

"What is your mother's name?"

"Xoco, but she died when I was born."

"I share your grief," I replied automatically.

"It's all right," Chumana replied. "I don't remember her."

"Did you serve Lady Katarina when she was here at the Green Lady earlier this afternoon?"

"Yes, m'lady."

"Did you mention a strange woman who tried to use the tunnel from the Green Lady to Love?"

"Yes, m'lady." Chumana gulped. "I thought the story would amuse her because she grew up at Love."

"Would you please describe the strange woman to me?"

Chumana scrunched her little face as she recalled the information. So far, her skin color hadn't changed one bit, other than during her initial fear that she was in trouble with the Temples.

"She was here three nights ago when it rained. She dressed like a guardswoman. Leather jerkin and leggings, white cotton tunic. A green oiled cloak to keep her dry. It was funny because she tried to use the passage to Love. Course, the sisters blocked it up last winter, and everyone, but visitors who hadn't been here recently, know that."

Chumana paused from her story to breathe. "Anyway, she was cursing up a storm, and I told her Father doesn't allow that kind of language in the inn. That's when Harold the Wagoneer told her he could entertain her better than the sisters. She drew her knife, and I told her Father didn't let people stab each other either no matter how rude they were. That's when she started laughing and her hood fell back and she put her knife away."

The girl cocked her head and examined me. "She had blue-black hair like yours except it was curly. In fact she looked a lot like you, except for your red eyes and bigger nose."

Shi Hua giggled at Chumana's description of me. I ignored the sister of Light.

"Did this stranger ask you about Orrin's tunnel system?" I said.

"Yes, m'lady." Chumana nodded vigorously. "I told her it would be easier for her to go straight to the Temple, but she wasn't having none of that. I said she wouldn't be able to get into the tunnels to go to Love since the duke and the magistrate and the wardens guarded all the outside entrances unless she went to one of the other Temples. That's when she raised her hand like she were going to strike me. Harold grabbed her wrist and said I wasn't smarting off. That I was telling the truth."

"Chumana! Why didn't you tell me a custom attempted to strike you?" Alo blurted.

The girl shrugged. "Because she didn't actually do it. She laughed some more before she gave me a strange coin. She told me to donate it to the Temples next time I went to services. It weren't even a proper queen's copper though."

"Do you still have the coin?" I asked.

She nodded and dug into the pocket of her apron. "I kept it with me since Father and I attend services at the Temple of Thief on First Day." She handed me the coin.

Pewter. Approximately the size of a queen's copper. Since it had been in Chumana's possession for a few days, there as no way even Luc could possibly lay a tracking spell on the coin.

I ran my fingers over the surfaces. The symbol for Thief was stamped on one side with an "X" scratched over it. A strange glyph was on the other side, one neither Thief nor Knowledge had learned the meaning of since we'd first encountered it. I often wondered if it was a symbol in the demon's language.

However, no magic, human or demon, contaminated the metal. I slid the coin across the table for Shi Hua to examine it. A glimmer of her distaste batted against my psyche.

"So, is she now officially a member, or simply delivering a message?" The Light priestess passed the object to her warden.

Mateqai examined the pewter coin before he handed it over to Little Bear. "Maybe she's here to prove her worth to them."

"To who?" Alo asked.

"The Assassins Guild," I murmured as I waited for my chief warden's opinion. The innkeeper gasped, but poor Chumana appeared confused.

Little Bear gave the coin back to me. "I would agree with Warden Mateqai at this point. Happenstance is the only reason the high sister isn't lying in Death's morgue."

I held up the pewter coin. "May I buy this token from you, Chumana?"

"You may have the cursed thing, Lady Justice," Alo blurted.

His daughter had a better mind for business. She lifted her chin. "Ten coppers."

"I was going to offer a silver." I smiled at the girl.

Her mouth opened and closed before she finally said, "Deal."

I drew a silver coin from a hidden pocket in my robes and handed it to her.

She bobbed her head. "Thank you, Lady Justice. Do you have any other questions for me?"

"Not at the moment," I said. "However, I suggest you do not repeat the story of the strange woman or my visit with you to anyone else. It may put yours and your father's lives in terrible danger."

"I swear I won't say another word 'bout it, m'lady." Chumana nodded gravely.

"Wh-what should we do if the woman comes back?" Alo asked, his fearful gaze flipping between me and Shi Hua.

"Send Chumana to the Jing Embassy," Shi Hua said. "It's closer to your inn than the Temples. My Lord Ambassador will protect your daughter at my request, and he will be able to contact me without revealing anything to the assassin."

Shi Hua released the truthspell on Chumana while I drew down the wards. I held out more coins to Alo as we all rose to our feet.

"Thank you for your hospitality, Master Innkeeper," I said as he accepted the payment for the tankards. "I hope I will have adequate time some day to more thoroughly enjoy it."

"We're here to serve, Lady Justice," he replied with a bow.

As we exited the inn, Shi Hua asked, "What next?"

I mounted Nassa and looked at the sister. "I have a convocation to deal with this evening. I suggest you visit you kinswoman and seek her advice on the coming arrival."

Shi Hua nodded, and she and Mateqai headed down the cross street that was Embassy Row.

"Ambassador Quan's going to hold this over your head," Little Bear muttered.

"Of that, I have no doubt." I shook my head. "It's a sad day when I trust a foreign prince more than my own sisterhood."

Chapter 8

My staff were their usual efficient selves. When Little Bear and I returned from the Green Lady, Sivan already had tables set in a triangular pattern in the courtroom. Unneeded benches and the accused's box had been stacked neatly in the gallery.

Technically, this would be the fifth convocation amongst the Orrin clergy in less than five months when we normally only had one per year. However, it was the first one I called. I wasn't sure what that portended, but it couldn't be anything good.

I took my dinner in my office while I reviewed Yanaba's decisions from today's court session. A little relief crept into my soul. All of the cases involved Orrin's usual problems from this time of year, in other words petty thefts and a couple of bar brawls from the insane heat we were having.

Yanaba was definitely coming into her own. There was little I could instruct her on anymore. She should have her own seat.

Assuming we could safely break her bond with the city itself.

If we couldn't, it was entirely possible for the Reverend Mother to assign me to another city within the queendom. And it would mean I would be parted from Luc. Probably for the rest of our lives.

Sivan drew a cool bath for me, and I used it to drown my fears of the future. If it weren't for the threats of both the Assassins Guild and a demon incursion, I would try to talk Luc into visiting the little cove between Orrin and Nastine for a day. We spent many an afternoon swimming there when we rode circuit.

However much I wanted to stay in my bath for the rest of the evening, I couldn't. When I dried off and entered my bedchamber, I was surprised to find Sivan had laid out a formal cotton chiton instead of the utilitarian leggings and tunic Temple uniform I preferred. She must have snuck it in when she replaced my clothing after Yanaba had activated the Balance defenses during the spring demon infiltration and destroyed nearly everything in the Temple along with the demons.

"What point are you trying to make?" I growled.

"It's the point you need to make," she smoothly as she retrieved a silver belt from my wardrobe. "Would you prefer sandals or bare feet this evening?"

"I'd prefer a sturdy pair of boots," I grumbled.

Sivan glared at me. "Are you planning to stomp people in the head like your mother?"

Her deliberate rudeness stunned me for a moment.

When I could breathe again, I said, "I don't like walking helpless into any crowd."

"If you go to the convocation you called and held in your own Temple, while armed to the teeth, it looks like you are planning to get rid of the rest of the seats whether that is your intention or not. You need to dress as befits your station as a chief justice of the third largest city in the Queendom of Issura. Not like a back country circuit traveling judge."

"You never would have spoken like this to Penelope—" I began.

"Because she was madder than a Rus berserker who had eaten tainted honey," Sivan bit out. "You need to be better than her."

"I could have you lashed—" I started again.

"Yes, you could." Sivan shook her head. "But I know you're smarter than Penelope, and you know I'm right."

"The first part of that statement is true," I said.

"You'll have your sword as the emblem of our Temple and your magic." Sivan pulled another item from the wardrobe. "Plus there's a ceremonial sheath that goes with the belt. I had it made to fit your favorite dagger."

I swallowed my pride. My head of household truly was doing her duty despite my whining. "Thank you, Sivan."

She sniffed. "Well, someone had to turn a brat of the Spring Rituals into a respectable lady justice. The Reverend Mother and her staff did a piss-poor job with you."

I glared at her.

Sivan raised an eyebrow. "A step too far?"

"Yes," I bit out before I sighed. "However, you are right about the Reverend Mother."

We both laughed. The humor smoothed a bit of edginess that had plagued me since this morning's time rewind. It had been bad enough when I learned Gerd had escaped a few weeks ago. The idea she was wandering at will through Orrin and no one but a child noticed . . .

"Sivan, when you're done with my hair—" I stepped into the chiton and pulled it up to my shoulders. "—please have Lailani draft a request to Alo of the Green Lady Inn and High Brother Luc to have Alo's daughter Chumana tested for talent."

My assistant stepped toward me to pin the garment at my shoulders with silver brooches. "What makes you think the girl has talent?"

"Because I believe Gerd has been moving through Orrin wearing some sort of glamour."

"Could it be Chumana simply was more observant than anyone else?" Sivan reached for the silver belt and sheath laying on my bed and fastened it about my waist.

"If Gerd's using demon magic like we suspect, it would explain why no one else noticed her." I held up my arms while Sivan fussed with the drape of my chiton over the belt. "She was the high sister of Love for twenty-five years. Someone would have recognized her. If Chumana can see through a demon glamour, such an ability could give us an edge for the next attack."

"You're assuming the general populace is that familiar with the seats of Orrin." Sivan made a final adjustment before she stepped back and examined her work. "She's been gone for nearly half a year, she was wearing civilian clothing, and the citizens have had far more to worry about than a renegade Love priestess."

"They pay more than enough attention to me," I grumbled.

Sivan clicked her tongue. "You, my dear Justice, stand out in a crowd. Now, have a seat so I don't need to fetch a ladder to style your hair for tonight."

Generally, I wore my hair in a single braid, wound and pinned to the back of my head. Over the years, I found the style the most efficient as far as time expenditure for the task and keeping it out of my way during a fight. First, Luc when we were on circuit, and then Sivan here at the Temple, wanted to do something more sophisticated.

Maybe it was a good thing I couldn't see my reflection in a mirror unless I borrowed someone else's vision. I was absolutely sure I looked ridiculous with all my hair curled and piled on top of my head. It was definitely heavy. I touched a ringlet only to have Sivan slap my hand away.

"Don't you dare ruin my work," she snapped. "For once, you look your station. Not like some sword for hire." She pulled a handkerchief off a tray of tiny pots. "Now hold still while I—"

I grabbed her wrist that had picked up a brush. "What the demon do you think are you doing?"

"There's other ways of intimidation than steel and spells, Chief Justice," she replied.

"So you're going to paint my face like a—" I stopped myself before I said anything inexcusable. My resentment toward Love had more to do with my birth mother, but the situation with Claudia was a close second.

"No, Anthea," Sivan murmured. "I want you to look like Balance Herself the day she warned humankind of the demons. The other seats need to take this seriously, and you would do well to use all of your talents, not just the ones the sisterhood at the home Temple taught you."

I released her wrist. "I apologize, Sivan. The demons and Gerd have me jumping at everything these days."

Sivan sighed. "Not just you, m'lady. I swear I'm going to use some cosmetic techniques the Kemet pharaohs use. And you can't tell me they look like the sister of Love attending worshippers."

"I wouldn't know," I said. For once, I was being straightforward instead of sarcastic. "I can't see any drawings or paintings of them."

"Do you trust me?"

I nodded, then held still as she applied the cosmetic paints and powders to my eyelids, cheeks, and lips.

Finally, she stood back to check the effect and smiled. "You look very formidable, Chief Justice."

"I feel like a doll you've dressed and painted for Ming Wei to play with," I grumbled.

Someone knocked on my bedchamber door. Sivan shot me an irritated look before she answered it. Nathan stood in the doorway in his formal livery. He stared at me.

"You look beautiful."

"Squire!" Sivan snapped. "Mind your place."

Nathan's face turned a brilliant scarlet, and he stammered but didn't make any sense.

No, he shouldn't have said what he did, but the gesture still warmed my heart. "Thank you for the compliment, Nathan. Did you come to tell me something?"

He audibly gulped. "Your guests have started to arrive, Chief Justice."

"Very well." I sighed. "The sooner we start, the sooner this will be over with." I strode to my weapons shelves and placed my dagger in my new sheath before I grabbed my sword and harness and buckled them on.

Little Bear and Gina stood outside of my bedchambers. They both blinked at my appearance, but then it was the first time either of them had seen me in something other than the standard Temple attire. They wore brand new uniforms. From the scent of polish, their boots and tack had been buffed until the items shone. They fell in step behind me and Nathan.

The sensation of walking through my Temple in my bare feet felt odd, almost as if I were constantly touching Yanaba, not bare marble. I hadn't noticed it before, but then the only times I didn't wear my boots was in my bath or my bed. I'd done enough spells in my bedchambers that my essence had soaked my rooms. But out here, it was definitely Yanaba's magic that penetrated my soles.

Maybe detaching her from Orrin itself would be impossible after all.

I followed Nathan into the courtroom. Luc and Talbert stood near the gallery railing, talking quietly. They both turned toward me when my escort and I entered. They gaped at me as if I were a demon.

"Good eventide, High Brothers." I stopped before them and inclined my head before I looked around me. My own wardens were staring at me, too. What the demon had Sivan done to my face? Ignoring them would be the best way for me to survive this convocation.

"Any luck tracking our visitor, High Brother Talbert?" I said.

He shook his head. "High Brother Jax is receiving the latest report from his second. High Brother Luc has been gracious enough to let us borrow Sister Shi Hua."

Which meant Jax's people were out of range for simple silent speech.

"I'll save my additional questions for the convocation." I put on a polite smile. "I do appreciate yours and High Brother Jax's assistance today. This morning's incident was a warning to all of us."

"We are here to serve, m'lady." Talbert bowed.

"Thank you, High Brother." I looked at Luc. "Will you both stay after the convocation? I fear there are some additional matters I need to discuss privately regarding a lead on the investigation."

Both men nodded.

High Brother Han entered the courtroom. I bowed to Talbert and Luc before I crossed the room to greet the High Brother of Conflict.

I continued to greet the other seats as they arrived. Most of them were surprised by my manners as much as my appearance, though High Brother Ben of Vintner seemed distant and preoccupied when I spoke with him. Even High Father Jerrod was coolly cordial. The only issue was the new seat of Mother.

High Mother Leocadia glared at me from the moment she entered the courtroom. She had been transferred to Orrin from Gilwas. Even though the remaining priestesses from Bianca's reign weren't involved in her predecessor's child selling scheme, their stories about me and the incident hadn't helped my attempts to establish a professional relationship with Leocadia.

I approached her. The crackle of her magic felt more like an out-of-control inferno than the welcome warmth of a cook fire. I inclined my head.

"Thank you for coming tonight, High Mother."

"Did I have a choice?" she snapped.

"We all have choices," I said. "It's a question if we've thought through the consequences of our choices."

"And do you?"

I resisted the urge to sigh. Rising to Leocadia's bait wouldn't help any potential relationship between us.

"I try to." I waved around the room. "As do our fellow seats. High Father Jerrod, the one person here who has every right to despise me, still came because he knows we cannot afford to be enemies. Not with demons on the march again, and those within the Temples who aid them."

"Are you saying that is the case with Mother?" Leocadia looked as if she wanted to strike me.

"Our chief justice is very much aware it is my Temple that has produced the most problems," Luc interjected as he approached us.

"And every Temple has been infiltrated, including Balance," I added. "None of our orders is immune from corruption." The bells began ringing Second Evening. "If you have any other questions, I hope you'll ask them during this convocation."

With a polite nod to Leocadia, Luc and I moved to our places at the base of the triangle in front of the statue of Balance Herself. I drew my sword and banged the pommel on the table surface.

"Let us begin."

I set my sword before me and perched on the edge of my chair. Dragonfly sat to my right while High Brother Han of Conflict took the seat to Luc's left. Once everyone was settled, my wardens closed all the doors to the courtroom as they departed.

Everyone's color showed various shades of worry. Everyone except Ben and Leocadia. Her irritation made sense, but his color was a pale yellow. Was he coming down with an illness? It would explain Ben's distracted manner earlier. However, any concern for his wellbeing needed to wait.

"I've called this convocation because the matter relates to our mid-winter convocation. Gerd, the former high sister of Love, has escaped from custody," I stated.

Only Leocadia was surprised by the news. "Why wasn't she tried and executed months ago?"

"That's a very good question," I said. "One I haven't received an answer for. At this point, I have to assume my own Reverend Mother is gravely embarrassed which is why she won't give me an answer. Outside of the home Temples, Queen Teodora, and the queen's council, the news is only known by the Temples of Orrin, Magistrate DiCook, and Duke Marco."

"I'm assuming this has to do with the death at Love this morning," High Sister Mariana of Knowledge said.

I nodded. "The Reverend Mother of Love believed Gerd might come back to Orrin given her irrational thinking and the lack of remorse for her crimes. We have proof Gerd was in Orrin for two of the last three days. However, we have an even greater problem." Luc's love steadied and supported my own emotions. "The guards at the north cove entrance to the tunnel system were killed with demon magic sometime between the change of personnel at First Night and when the murder was discovered a candlemark before First Morning."

A hiss of dismay went through my fellow seats who didn't already know this. Again, the only one not to react to my news was Ben. I swallowed my own discomfort and continued.

"The murders were how Gerd accessed the tunnel entrance to Love. At this point in the investigation, we don't know who actually performed the demon magic, but we need to assume the demons have been teaching the renegades."

I glanced at Dragonfly, but she stared at her clasped hands resting on the table top. "By happenstance, High Sister Dragonfly had been called from her chambers to attend Sister Claudia. Unfortunately, High Sister Dragonfly's head of household Gregorios entered her chambers to prepare her bath, and Gerd killed them."

Several of the assemblage murmured the ritual words of shared grief. High Sister Mya of Child reached over and laid her hand on Dragonfly's clutched fingers. A whisper of Mya's talent raised the fine hairs on my bare arms as she lent her strength to Dragonfly.

"According to what information we do have, Gerd seeks revenge on myself and Dragonfly for her downfall—" I stopped speaking when High Brother Ben of Vintner abruptly stood.

He walked past Xander, but Ben's steps were stumbling as if he'd sampled too much of his own Temple's products. He drew his knife while taking two more halting steps. That's when the alien touch of demon magic seeped past my mental shields.

Chapter 9

"Stop Ben!" I shouted as I surged to my feet. "He's being controlled by demon magic!"

At the same time, Yanaba cried out in my mind, *Demon magic in the temple!*

Xander grabbed Ben from behind while Jerrod dove under the table. Leocadia rushed to assist Xander, but Ben continued to stagger forward. Han jumped up and added his strength to Xander's to keep the knife away from anyone's flesh. Twelve help us. With the alliance between the renegades and the Assassins Guild, the odds were the blade was coated in poison.

"Luc!"

But his eyes were closed, and he was mumbling under his breath. Thunder cracked inside the walls, and the floor shivered beneath my soles. I slapped my hands over my ears, as did most of the other clergy. Others squeezed their eyes shut.

Ben, however, appeared to be waking from a deep sleep. "Wha—" He blinked a few times. "What is going on?"

Wardens from all the Temples rushed in through every doorway except the one leading to our empty gaol. Little Bear raced to my side as Wardens Dezba and Tahoma disarmed Ben and took control of him, though he no longer struggled the holds on his arms.

"What the demon is going on in here, Chief Justice?" Little Bear demanded. "It sounded like someone lit a keg of Jing flash powder."

"Part of it was my fault," Luc said before he looked up at me. "I've been reading through Kam's journals. He created a spell during his novice years that replicates the effects of a flashbang. He also used it to break a mind-control spell affecting a group of citizens in Nastine. I gambled it might work on High Brother Ben before someone got stabbed."

"Stabbed?" Ben looked at Luc with a puzzled expression. "Who got stabbed?"

Something's wrong with Mya, Yanaba whispered in my mind. Of course, she would pick up on the seat of Child. The two women's spells had been interlinked when demons wearing human skins infiltrated Balance.

"Mya?" I looked at the High Sister of Child. Her skin had turned to a similar pale yellow as Ben's had been a moment before. "Mya, are you all right?"

"I will be." Her smile was weak. Talbert stood by her side and held her, no doubt to extend his quicksilver abilities to block the emotional wash of everyone in the courtroom in addition to the physical support.

"Do you need some rest before assisting me in examining our brother of Vintner?" I asked. Her health still concerned me, though with Talbert's efforts, her color was warming to a golden color.

"No, but I will need privacy to examine him."

"Examine me? For what?" Ben looked around the assembled seats and wardens, including Jerrod who finally crawled from underneath the table. Leocadia looked at her counterpart with a disgusted expression.

"Would our reception room be adequate, High Sister?"

"Yes, thank you." Mya inclined her head to me.

What the demon is going on? Yanaba said silently.

The wardens have everything under control now. Give me a few moments to get the convocation sorted, I replied. *Please check on Elizabeth.*

All right. Thankfully, Yanaba didn't throw a fit about not being included. She understood her primary duty right now was to protect the child she carried.

I looked at Vintner's chief warden and reached out with my senses, but no taint of demon magic surrounded him. "Chief Warden Mangas, has a warden been stationed inside the high brother's bedchambers every night?"

The man blinked, but I wasn't sure if he was confused by my inquiry because I barked a question at him when I had no authority over him, or the fact my wardens were guiding his charge out of the courtroom.

"I've followed the joint recommendations," Mangas finally said. "Warden Golden Eagle was posted in the high brother's rooms last night. He didn't report anything unusual. Do you wish to speak with him?"

"Yes, but please stay here." I looked at Little Bear. He nodded and whispered to Noko, who had joined my little group at our table. She darted out of the courtroom's main doors. The color of Mangas's skin shifted from bright orange to a dull yellow. At first, I feared he'd been enspelled as well, but since his skin didn't change toward any greenish hues, he was probably more upset I didn't trust him.

I didn't blame him for his emotional reaction, but my trust was in short supply at the moment.

"Warden Long Feather and Warden Ahiga, would you please escort Chief Warden Mangas to our ready room and get him some refreshment?" Little Bear looked the Vintner warden in the eye. "I'll come for you when the chief justice is ready to talk to you."

Mangas merely nodded to his counterpart and walked out with the two Balance wardens.

I rapped the pommel of my sword against the table. My action silenced everyone in the room. Luc looked up at me with a worried expression, but he said nothing silently or otherwise.

"My fellow clergy, I don't think we have a choice any longer." I took a steadying breath. "The renegades are using the damn tunnel system against us, just like they did to the Temples in Tandor. All of you need to destroy the spells to access the tunnels from your Temples. I'll contact the Mining Guild in the morning about safely collapsing the exits outside the city walls. Do any of you object to this plan of action?"

No one said a word. Not even High Mother Leocadia.

"Do any of you need assistance beyond your own wardens?" I asked.

There was a chorus of negations.

I nodded. "Is there anything else we need to address tonight?"

The remaining seats shook their heads.

"Let me add one last thing," I said. "The Assassins Guild may have helped Gerd escape. They are in league with the renegades and the demons. She's in Orrin to redeem herself in her allies' eyes, and she will take out as many of us as she can to earn that redemption. Please take any precautions you feel are necessary at your own Temples."

"Chief Justice, should we warn the populace?" High Sister Mariana of Knowledge said, her voice laced with worry and fear.

I hesitated a fraction. Mariana was merely suggesting a logical course of action. And Gerd wouldn't hesitate to kill little Chumana, or even my squires, if she thought they were a danger to her.

Or if she knew she could hurt me by doing so.

"We of the Temples are Gerd and her allies' targets." I inhaled deeply before I continued. "The duke and the magistrate are aware of the attack at Love. Right now, we would only be frightening the populace of Orrin unnecessarily by issuing a warning, especially after the near riot a few weeks ago in the South Side."

Mariana nodded.

"Anyone else have a question or concern?" I scanned all the faces in the room, but other than their general fear and worry pounding against my shields, no one added anything. If the emotions in the room were making my head ache, I couldn't imagine how Mya was still upright. "Thank you for coming to the convocation and good eventide." I banged the pommel of my sword once against the tabletop before I sheathed it.

While nearly everyone shuffled out the main doors, Leocadia's attention flicked to Jerrod and back to me. So, it wasn't just the priestesses at Mother telling stories about me. And Jerrod's behavior tonight had set back the high mother's estimation of him. She approached me and inclined her head.

"I owe you an apology, Chief Justice," she murmured.

"No, High Mother." I shook my head. "No, you don't."

"Very well then. Send for me if you need assistance." She bowed. "I am here to serve." Leocadia whirled on her heel to leave, her robes flaring. The new chief warden of Mother fell in step beside her as they exited my Temple.

That was a swift change in her attitude, Luc said silently. *Jerrod's bravery truly impressed her.*

What was that lecture you gave me about not making sarcastic comments concerning the other seats? I replied.

Talbert and Mya approached us. The corners of the high brother's mouth twitched, the closest he came to a grin. "I'm assuming Ben wasn't the reason you wanted to speak with me at the end of the convocation."

"No." I sighed. "But he is the issue we need to deal with first."

The rest of the seats had departed, except Jax. He hung back while I spoke with Talbert, but from his fidgeting, it was obvious he had something to say. I waved him over.

"I did not wish to interrupt, Chief Justice," the Wildling priest murmured. "However, you should know my people lost Gerd's scent in the town of Redwood Grove."

It wasn't a surprise. In fact, I was shocked the Wildlings managed to follow her that far. Redwood Grove was a fair-sized town, bigger than Nastine. It was nestled on a plateau in the foothills of the Grey Mountains near the border between the duchies of Orrin and Pana.

However, something didn't make sense. Redwood Grove was a day's ride only at a full gallop with the rider changing horses along the way. It had been on mine and Luc's circuit.

I shook my head. "Your second is an excellent tracker, but Gerd could not make it that far in that amount of time."

Jax chuckled. "Sister Farrah said the same thing. Thank you for allowing Sister Shi Hua to assist us, High Brother." He bowed to Luc. "I hope we did not overtire her."

A wry grin spread across Luc's face. "I'm sure Warden Mateqai would have informed you thusly if you had."

Jax turned back to me. "As you hinted, there is no way to reach Redwood Grove on two legs in that length of time. We suspect we were led on a merry chase, just as we were when the skinwalker abducted Luc last winter. Knowing Gerd, she set a trap for you."

"Which begs the question, why does she want Anthea out of the city?" Mya murmured.

My warden Noko entered the courtroom followed by High Brother Han and his own warden. From the brilliant color of the skin of all three, I knew what had happened before Noko opened her mouth.

"Golden Eagle is dead, Chief Justice," she spat. "We found him hanging by the neck from the grape trellis in the Vintner's garden."

Chapter 10

I swore under my breath at Noko's news. It meant either Golden Eagle had been recruited by the renegades or Gerd had bespelled the Vintner warden in order to get to High Brother Ben.

"You should have stayed there and had Vintner send—" I started.

"Is Warden Daniel still there?" Little Bear interjected.

Noko nodded.

Regret washed through me. Of course, Little Bear would have ordered her to take a backup to Vintner. "I apologize, Warden. I shouldn't have made assumptions."

"Apology accepted." A wry smile tilted her mouth. "High Brother Xander is already on his way there. I met him and High Brother Han on the street on my way back here. We cut Golden Eagle down to check his pulse and breathing, but . . ." She swallowed hard. "Other than that, we've touched nothing and kept the Vintner wardens and staff from interfering with anything around the scene."

"Thank you," I said. Xander and his chief warden would support Daniel in protecting anything regarding the death from further contamination.

"What assistance do you need from us?" Han rumbled.

"Would you accompany Luc down to Vintner?" I hated the next thing I was about to say when I looked at him. "Do you want Elizabeth or Yanaba?"

He frowned. "Yanaba does not need the additional stress when she's finally eating again. Jeremy or Garbhan?"

"I fear we need to speed up young Brother Garbhan's training," I murmured.

"How may I serve?" Jax asked. He wore his wide grin that meant he was enjoying the current chaos.

Or rather, he sought an excuse to sink his teeth into an unwary foe.

"Would you mind staying here with me while Brother Garbhan and I question Chief Warden Mangas and High Brother Ben after High Sister Mya examines him?" I said.

"Not at all, Chief Justice." If anything, Jax's grin widened.

Using his crutches, Luc leveraged himself to stand on his right foot. "Do you wish someone from the Healers Guild to examine the corpse?"

"Yes, please." I sighed. "If the master healer who attends desires a further examination at the guild house, send a messenger for me."

"Of course, Chief Justice," Luc murmured.

Wardens Gina and Noko entered the courtroom, escorting Elizabeth. I quickly relayed the facts to my sister justices through silent speech. She said nothing about the task I gave Yanaba, but then, Elizabeth had been chief justice of Tandor far longer than I had been of Orrin. She would understand the need to give all Temple personnel tasks to perform in a crisis.

"I'm ready when you are, good sirs," Elizabeth said.

Luc inclined his head as did Han. The two priests headed for my Temple's main doors with their own wardens in tow. Elizabeth and the two Balance wardens followed. Han was insisting they ride as they exited. However, Luc and Elizabeth were having none of Han's coddling.

Jax chuckled. "Will High Brother Han survive the trip to Vintner?"

"Not if he keeps pestering Justice Elizabeth," I said.

Jax shook his head. "I've seen Light's clergy in their practice yard.

High Brother Luc may have lost an appendage, but he has taken Sister Shi Hua and her kinswoman's lessons to heart."

My body stiffened at Jax's admission.

He cocked his head. "Her scent gives her away. No one beyond my brothers and sisters know, Chief Justice."

"I'm not the one to be worried about, High Brother." I scowled at Jax to make my point. "Ambassador Quan would be most wroth should anyone learn of his concubine's relationship to Sister Shi Hua or of said concubine exercising with High Brother Luc. We cannot afford to lose our source of flash powder."

"Understood, m'lady." Jax bent his head, thereby showing his neck to me.

For the life of me, I had a terrible time figuring out Wildlings. On one hand, they were less adept at the social graces than I was. On the other hand, they were honest to a fault.

I turned to Mya and Talbert, both of whom had waited patiently through the successive chaos. "How would you like to proceed, High Sister?"

"You reception room will do fine." Her attention flicked to Talbert and back. "I know you'll want to observe my examination of Ben. Will you and Jax be willing to let Talbert extend his quicksilver shield over you so I can work?"

"I have no issue." I looked at Jax. "Do you have an objection, High Brother?"

"None," he answered.

"Then let us get this taken care of before I'm summoned to the Healers Guild," I grumbled.

I resembled a mother duck as I headed toward our little reception room with Little Bear at my side and the other seats and their wardens following. Jonata guarded the door, and she opened it as we approached.

Ben slumped in a chair. His skin still wasn't back to normal, but it no longer had the sickly look of a skinwalker. Dezba and Tahoma stood at opposite ends of the room, watching the seat of Vintner.

"High Brother, High Sister Mya needs to examine your mind," I said.

"I don't understand how I ended up in Balance with a knife in my hand," Ben murmured.

"I can't do this with everyone in here," High Sister Mya said. "The wardens need to leave."

Her statement triggered a loud chorus of denials by all the wardens, but Little Bear's voice cut through them all. "I most certainly will not leave the chief justice alone in here after what happened during the convocation!"

"Chief Warden, the high sister needs quiet to perform her examination." I glared at Little Bear. "High Brother Talbert can't shield all of you. Between my sword and High Brother Jax's claws, I think we can protect ourselves and High Sister Mya."

Little Bear opened his mouth to protest. Instead, he sucked in a deep breath and released it.

I'll be careful. I promise, I said silently.

He trembled slightly at the touch of my mind against his. I knew how much he disliked silent speech, and I rarely did it, but the fact I did so now relayed the importance of this situation far more than my shouting would have. He nodded in acquiescence.

"What do you wish me to do with High Brother Ben's knife?" Tahoma held out the weapon. He had the forethought to wrap the knife with silk to keep his essence from contaminating it.

"There's something oily on the blade," Little Bear reported.

I muttered a Cantan curse under my breath. My suspicion the blade had been poisoned was probably right. "Do you have something ceramic to store it in?"

"Yes. Let me have it." Little Bear held out his right hand, and Tahoma carefully handed it over by the handle. "I'll lock it in my office until you have a moment to examine it."

The other wardens gave Little Bear a wide berth as he strode out of the room.

"The rest of you—out," Mya ordered.

There was a lot of grumbling from the wardens, especially Mya's own chief warden, but they all left. I knew Dezba and Tahoma would be guarding the doors to the reception room while I was in it. Little Bear would have their hides if they didn't.

I closed the doors behind the exodus of wardens and turned to Mya. "Do you want me to ward the room?"

She nodded.

"Will Anthea's wards stand if she's surrounded by Talbert's shields?" Jax asked.

"Inside Balance, yes," Talbert said. "I'll only be a shield for your emotions, not your magic."

I drew my sword once again and walked the perimeter of the room, muttering the incantation. No one could enter the room or hear anything within while my wards stood. Since this was Mya's examination of Ben's mental state, it didn't require a clerk to record the proceedings.

However, Little Bear would summon Donella as my senior clerk, and she would be waiting outside with her paper, ink, and quills for the formal interrogation I would have to do after Mya was finished with Ben. I sheathed my sword and stood a pace away from the Wilding priest.

At Mya's nod, Talbert released her hand, stepped between me and Jax and placed a hand on each of our shoulders. The effect of his shields was similar to sticking my head underwater. Instead of dulling sound, it dulled the presence of the other people in the room. I scored above normal in empathy, but I could immediately feel why Mya seldom left Child and why she enlisted Talbert's aid when she did. Frankly, I'd go mad if I were trapped inside of Balance.

I also understood what exactly had happened to Yanaba when she piggybacked her spell on top of Mya's tracking spell. My junior justice's talents had been expanded and shifted to the Child style. It explained why she couldn't leave the city. The magical interaction had altered Yanaba's psyche.

Probably permanently.

Mya sat next to Ben. "Give me your hand."

He did so, but he also shook his head. "I don't know how much good you can do. Even if Anthea truthspells me, I don't remember what happened between going to bed last night and waking up in Balance's courtroom."

"Then don't try to remember." Mya smiled softly. "Let me do the work. Close your eyes. I'll count to ten, and you take a breath and release it with each number."

Ben's eyelids fluttered shut. Mya softly and slowly counted. He inhaled deeply and released the air. His pulse at his throat and wrists slowed.

"Can you hear me, Ben?" she said soothingly.

"Yes."

"It is last night. Who is walking with you down the corridor to your bedchambers?"

"Sister Nina and Chief Warden Mangas."

"Are they talking with you?" Mya asked. Her eyes had closed as well, and her voice took on an odd cadence.

"Yes." Ben frowned. "Sister Nina reported a vial of soma powder and a bottle of qunubu extract were missing from our stores. Chief Warden Mangas said he would begin an investigation. He requested leave to ask Chief Justice Anthea for assistance. He was concerned someone within Vintner was the culprit."

"What else did you discuss?" Mya prompted.

"Mangas said Golden Eagle would be standing watch in my bedchambers tonight." Ben sighed. "I have such a hard time sleeping with the wardens in the room. Their presence impinges on my subconscious, and I have such odd dreams."

"Did either the sister or the chief warden say anything more?" Mya asked.

"No."

"Did Golden Eagle say anything to you?"

"He merely wished me pleasant dreams before he shielded his lantern."

Part of me wished I had Ben under a truthspell while Mya was talking to him. The other part of me wondered if he had been possessed. However, no miasma of a skinwalker oozed out of him. Or did I miss it when I flinched from Luc's spell version of a flashbang?

"You mentioned odd dreams," Mya continued. "Did you have an odd dream last night?"

Once again, Ben sighed. A sad expression fell over his features. I wish I knew what emotions he was truly experiencing.

"Ilina was in my bedchambers."

Grief swept over Mya's face. Talbert, Jax, and I exchanged looks. Sister Ilina of Love had died of the wasting disease two winters ago. Her daughter Katarina was now Duke Marco's wife. From what both Katarina and High Sister Dragonfly told me, Ilina was the one person besides me Gerd feared. Gerd didn't start killing and replacing Love's wardens until after Ilina's death. And after she kicked Katarina out on the streets.

Ilina and Ben? I asked.

Talbert and Jax both nodded.

Events and motives clicked in my mind. Gerd had stolen the soma tears and the qunubu, cast a glamour to appear as the dead sister, and used poor Ben's grief against him. Fury at the depths of my birth mother's depravity flooded me. I don't know why I was surprised considering the things she'd done in the past. This transgression was mild by comparison.

"What did Ilina do in your dream?" Mya asked gently.

"Sh-she disrobed and climbed on top of me." Ben trembled. "I knew it couldn't be her, but I missed her so much."

"Was Warden Golden Eagle there?"

"Y-yes. He was asleep on the floor." Ben gasped. "She said it was better that no one know she came to visit me." He sobbed. "I wanted it to be Ilina. I missed her so much. But it wasn't her."

"How do you know, Ben?" Mya stroked the back of his hand she held while keeping her eyes closed.

"She didn't smell like Ilina. She didn't move like Ilina." He shook his head. "I-I tried to shove her off me, to shout for the wardens. But her magic felt so alien. Unnatural. Not of this world. She did something to my spirit. I tried to fight her—"

Ben jerked in his seat. "Gerd. That bitch! How dare she—"

Mya screamed, but it was one of rage, not pain or fear.

The Vintner high brother's eyes popped open, and he yanked his hand free from Mya's grip. "You shouldn't have—shouldn't have—I'm so sorry you had to relive—"

"It's all right, Ben. I'm all right. And you will be, too." Mya swiped at the red tears running down her pale yellow cheeks. She looked over at me. "Gerd's definitely using demon magic. I can confirm she did on Ben."

"Do you need to do anything else before Talbert releases me from his shield?" I asked.

Mya smiled despite the tears still trickling down her face. "Just give him a chance to cover me before you release your wards."

"Of course," I said.

The instant Talbert retracted his quicksilver shields, Ben's fury and grief slammed against my psyche. I stumbled. As did Jax. Part of me was glad I wasn't the only one impacted by Ben's raw emotions.

Talbert strode over to Mya and rested his hands on her shoulders. She leaned her head against him, and her body relaxed.

"Ben?" I crossed to his chair and knelt beside him though I didn't touch him. He seemed brittle, as if he'd shatter from the slightest contact. "What do you need before I lower the wards?"

He swallowed hard. "I don't think your mother's head on a platter is an acceptable request."

I laughed. I couldn't help it. "You can always ask. I'll do my best to provide it."

He stared at me. "How can you laugh at all the chaos she's caused?"

"Because if I don't, I'll vomit." I gestured at the massive rug on the floor. "My head of household is already perturbed about all the messes I've been leaving on her spotless furnishings she's had to replace over the last few months."

My attempt at humor drew a weak smile from Ben.

"I appreciate your offer, m'lady," he said. "However, I believe I'd like to return to my own Temple and destroy the tunnel entrance in my bedchambers."

I rose to my feet. With a few words, my wards dropped. A thrum of magic pulsed under my bare soles with the distinctive heat from the hearth of Mother.

"At least, one of the seats is taking my warning seriously," I murmured.

"If the rest of us can go back to our Temples, we'll destroy our tunnel entrances." Jax wore a wide grin. "But of course, we're merely assuming Gerd has left Orrin."

And we needed to know where she was. If only my own Reverend Mother had tried and executed Gerd in a little more timely manner, we wouldn't be in this position. Dragonfly had already tried to give me Gerd's personal possessions, at least those not related to her charges. It wasn't legal for me to take Gerd's personal effects while she was still alive—

"I'm such an idiot!" I shouted.

I prayed to Balance my lack of focus didn't result in more people dying.

Chapter 11

The other four seats stared at me as if I'd lost my mind. Perhaps I had.

"Mya, will you be all right if Talbert takes you back to your Temple?" All pretense at manners and civility disappeared.

She nodded.

I turned to Jax. "Would you be willing to stay here with Ben and Mangas until I get back?"

"Of course, Anthea, but where—"

I dashed for the doors of the reception room and threw them open. "Little Bear! With me!"

Brother Garbhan and his warden escort was entering Balance as I raced out.

"Stay with Jax until I get back!" I didn't pause for an answer from the Light priest. My feet took the marble steps two at a time. Little Bear's boots pounded next to me.

Part of me was gratified he wasn't questioning me at the moment. If I was right, Gerd was still within the city walls.

Fine powder coated the cobblestones, making my balance on the boulevard tenuous at best. Even the streetcleaners couldn't stop the accumulation of dust during the dry season. I should have paused to pull on my own boots, but dirty feet didn't matter. I could only pray to the Twelve Dragonfly had put Gerd's personal belongings in a place my mother didn't know of or couldn't access.

Another thrum of power seeped through my soles, the white hot heat and sharp tang of a forge. Mother and Father, the two I expected the biggest arguments from, ended up being the first two passageways closed.

A third thrum. This time, it had the feel of the sun on my skin. Light. Luc must have ordered Jeremy to destroy the spell for their Temple on his way to Vintner. It reminded me I was remiss in my duty as well.

Yanaba?

What's happening? I'm feeling magic from the other Temples. Concern flowed through the link with my junior justice.

Do you have the strength to go to my bedchambers and destroy the spell to open the passageway to the tunnel system? Don't risk your child. Otherwise, Elizabeth or I will do it when we get back. Silent speech didn't steal any air as I ran, one of the many reasons I was grateful for that particular talent.

I can do it without risking the babe. A small tickle in my mind indicated she was laughing. *What did you do to get the seats to listen to you? Threaten them with a knife?*

Actually, that would be High Brother Ben brandishing a knife at a convocation, not me. Keep an ear out for things at Balance for me.

I'll go to the reception room after I take care of the passageway spell, Yanaba assured me.

A fourth pulse of power, one that smelled of dusty paper and parchment tinged with the metallic odor of ink. Knowledge magic. My feet pounded against the cobblestones. Gerd would be feeling the pulses, too. She'd know we were up to something. We needed to find her before she really did escape Orrin.

I didn't have to push my way past the revelers at Love. A murmur passed through the crowd waiting to worship with the priestesses. I wasn't wearing my traditional hood. My red eyes did all the work of getting people out of my way. Sister Claudia, flanked by two wardens, rushed over to me and Little Bear in their waiting area.

"Chief Justice—"

"Need to see the high sister now. Emergency," I said between great gasping breaths. Now that I wasn't riding circuit, I was sitting on my buttocks far too much, and it was beginning to show in my lack of endurance.

"This way." Dragonfly's second hurried toward the corridor leading to the priestesses' private quarters with me and our wardens following close behind.

She stopped and knocked on the door to the high sister's bedchambers.

Chief Warden Citana opened the door a crack and peered at us. "The High Sister is busy."

More power thrummed under my soles. It carried the softness of kitten feet coupled with the chill of a deep fog. Talbert must have also paused at Thief long enough to order his second Cedar Grove to destroy their passage to the tunnels.

I edged around Claudia. "It's imperative I speak with Dragonfly now, Chief Warden."

Citana's jaw dropped now that she could see my eyes beneath the lamp over the high sister's door. She stepped back from the entrance. I rushed across the sitting room and banged on the inner door to the bedchamber.

"Dragonfly! Open up! It's Anthea!" I listened for any sound of life before I pounded on the door again. "Dragonfly!"

Power thrummed through my body. Steel and the clean scent of a cloudless night on top of a mountain. Yanaba had done as I asked.

On its heels was another pulse of power. I grabbed the door latch to stay upright as sexual desire coursed through me. Claudia cried out behind me, but it wasn't one of pain or fear.

"Anthea." A man's voice. I whirled around, grabbed him, and kissed him.

"What the demon do you need . . ." Dragonfly's voice faded.

I jerked back from the person I kissed. Little Bear stared at me like I'd lost my damn mind. Maybe I had. Heat of another kind rushed through my body, and I hid my face in my hands.

"I'm so sorry, Chief Warden," I murmured.

Behind me, Dragonfly snickered. "When was the last time you were around Love magic, Anthea?"

"When I was three winters," I said through gritted teeth. To lose control of myself like that went beyond mere embarrassment.

Someone rested their hand on my shoulder. "What do you need, Anthea?"

I swallowed hard, lowered my hands, and tried not to look at my chief warden as I turned to face Dragonfly. "Gerd's belongings. You said you would store them until the final disposition of her case."

"Oh, demons take me!" she spat. "I am such a fool!" She pushed past me and stalked over to her desk. Metal rattled when she pull a ring of keys from the mass of ledgers still sitting there from this morning.

"Claudia, go back to your duties," she ordered. "I'll take care of this."

Her second nodded. "Good eventide, Chief Justice." Her robes fluttered as she pivoted and padded from the sitting room.

"Didn't your Reverend Mother take a lock of her hair?" Dragonfly beckoned us to follow her.

"That's standard procedure," I muttered.

"You didn't?"

"Yes, I did." The muscles of my face twitched. I had taken the requisite lock, but the Reverend Mother had taken it along with the cursed coins Gerd had used for Magistrate DiCook's bribe. She wanted all the evidence for Gerd's trial, and I hadn't questioned it because she was my superior.

A chill ran through me. Why hadn't the Reverend Mother used the lock to track Gerd when she escaped?

Dragonfly led me and our chief wardens to Love's kitchen. It was far larger than the space my cook commanded, but then Balance didn't entertain guests six nights of the week as Love did.

The staff was too busy to do more than incline their heads respectfully to their high sister and me. Apparently, the high sister traipsing through their domain didn't elicit questions the way my presence would in Balance.

Dragonfly opened a door. The puff of chill air confirmed the dark blue stairwell led to Love's cold room.

"You stored her belongings down here?" I asked.

Dragonfly gave an unladylike snort and led the way down the steps. The storage area at the bottom of the winding staircase was bigger than our cold room. With a start, I realized why. This was the equivalent of Balance's gaol or Death's morgue. And with the amount of foodstuffs Love's guests consume, the staff would need a much larger cold room.

She led us unerringly to the back where there were a set of shelves with nothing on them but five wooden boxes. She pulled out one in particular. "This one has her toiletry items."

I shivered. I didn't think I'd ever been in a cold room without wearing my regular uniform. My simple chiton wasn't heavy enough. It had been over a year now since I felt this chilled.

"Would you mind if we examine the contents upstairs?" My breath puffed across my face, yellow at first before shifting to green then blue before it dissipated

"Of course."

"Here, let me carry it, High Sister." Little Bear held out his hands.

"Would you like a kiss from me to reward you for your gallant behavior, Chief Warden?" A sly smile spread across Dragonfly's visage. My skin glowed as hot red as Little Bear's despite the biting air of the cold room.

"Your gratitude is more than sufficient, High Sister," he replied carefully.

Thankfully, Dragonfly didn't pursue the matter further. We followed her back up the winding staircase. This time, half the kitchen staff merely gave us curious looks. The rest were too busy with their duties to notice us.

Could Gerd have snuck into the Temple of Love via the kitchen? I didn't realize I'd voiced the question aloud until Citana said, "No."

"How can you be sure?" I murmured.

"We now have more wardens than the twelve formal ones," she said. When I looked at her, she shrugged. "Your Gina suggested it originally. The High Sister simply needs to decide which of the kitchen staff shall become her new head of household."

"And both the staff and the wardens are all right with this?" Little Bear asked.

"After what the renegades did to us, none of us have a problem with it," Dragonfly snarled.

Did Mya and her people know how deep Love's collective anger ran? Of course, she probably did, but it wouldn't be remiss of me to mention this conversation to Mya privately.

Once we were inside Dragonfly's sitting room, she directed Little Bear to set the box on the low table between the lounging couches. The table was made of ironwork filigree supporting a granite surface. Fine lines scored the center of the stone, radiating from the same point. Heat marks. Dragonfly had burned things on the surface before, probably for spellwork.

Citana locked the main doors before she strode across the room and closed the door to the bedchamber itself. Had Dragonfly not told her chief warden what she was doing in her bedchamber earlier? Or was Citana worried Gerd had cast some sort of spell to create another passage into the tunnels?

I knelt by the table, untied the piece of rope securing the lid, and opened the box. The scent of roses and sandalwood wafted from the items inside. Residue of the very expensive perfumes Gerd preferred.

For the briefest of instants, I was three winters again. Strangers were taking me away from the smells that had meant safety to a small child. When I broke free and stumbled toward her fragrance, she picked me up and thrust me away from her. "Take the brat if you want her so badly, Thalia."

Thalia.

So I had met my grandmother. At least once. She probably hadn't said a word to me about us being related. To do so would have gotten both herself and Kam executed.

I shuddered at the memory. Dragonfly knelt on the opposite side of the table and laid a hand on mine, but she said nothing. An unspoken understanding of the chaos and pain Gerd managed to inflict on everyone around her passed between us.

"We need a brush, a comb, a file," I said. "Anything with—"

"Residue from her body," Dragonfly replied. "Just because I haven't done a basic tracking spell since I was a novice, it doesn't mean I've forgotten everything I learned."

"I'm sorry." And I truly was. I hated feeling five steps behind the perpetrator I sought, and with my birth mother, the impression was constant.

"Her brush," Dragonfly said triumphantly. She pulled the grooming instrument from the box and plucked blue hairs from the equally blue bristles. Once she placed the brush back in the box, she waved Citana to remove it. Love's chief warden placed the box beside Dragonfly's desk.

Dragonfly placed the hairs on the table. When she looked at me, she lifted an eyebrow. "How do you wish to do this?"

Unease filled me. Bianca had been able to circumvent both my rewind and my tracking spell when I investigated the murder of an orphan boy a few weeks ago. How much illicit knowledge had the two co-conspirators exchanged? On the other hand, Gerd wouldn't have had time or forethought enough to sabotage any of her personal effects before Gina led a team of wardens to take over Love last winter.

I inhaled deeply in an effort to calm myself and released it. I couldn't put Dragonfly at risk regardless of my belief of relative safety. "I'll cast the spell. I need you to watch for any tricks Gerd might have laid on her belongings."

Dragonfly nodded.

I placed my palms flat on the stone tabletop. Sturdy, incorruptible granite. I concentrated, and my hands tapped the universal rhythm. Balance magic swirled around the hairs. A ribbon of energy danced and extended from the strands on the table, searching for its origin place.

The discordant beat I half-expected tried to seize my spell, but I fought it. Dragonfly's power melded with mine, strengthening the ribbon. The energy shot toward the closed and locked doors. It slipped through the narrow gaps.

The beat changed to a strange, guttural chittering. The language of demons. Alien magic blasted the tracking ribbon. The awful smell of burning hair flooded my nose.

"Fire!" Citana shouted.

I blinked out of my trance, but smoke stung my eyes. It wasn't just the strands Dragonfly plucked from Gerd's brush that were burning. White flames flickered from the box of my birth mother's personal effects.

And we were locked in the high sister's chambers.

Chapter 12

"Get the bath door open!" Little Bear roared. Citana dashed for the bedroom door. He snatched up the burning box and raced after his counterpart of Love. I scrambled to my feet while Dragonfly used the contents of a nearby decanter to extinguish the embers on her table.

"That felt like demon magic," she snapped as she stood.

"It was." I coughed from the acrid smoke. Twelve take my birth mother and cast her in the deepest pit they could find.

The rush of water came from deep in Dragonfly's quarters.

"The fire's out," Little Bear called out.

Muffled shouting came from out in the corridor before someone pounded on the main doors.

"High Sister! Fire in the Temple!" The voice could barely be heard over Temple bells clanging the emergency alarm.

Dragonfly muttered an obscenity under her breath. "Citana!"

The Love chief warden ran out of the bedchamber to the main doors. She unlocked them. I grabbed the pommel of my sword, but it was one of the new Love wardens.

"Fire in the kitchen, Chief Warden," the woman reported crisply. Her nose wrinkled when the smoke from Dragonfly's room registered. "We should evacuate—"

Citana shook her head. "Have the staff cover their noses and mouths before they take tubs of water down to the cold room. The burning items are four wooden boxes by themselves against the rear wall."

"How did you know?" The warden looked thoroughly confused, but her skin color faded to a light orange now that the initial alarm proved to be unneeded.

"Because the fifth box just caught fire in my chambers," Dragonfly snapped. "Do as the chief warden ordered. Please tell Sister Claudia to close the Temple and bestow tokens to those whose worship was interrupted. Tell the rest of the staff to open all the doors and use fans to clear the air in the Temple."

The warden jumped and scurried away.

Fury rolled from Dragonfly when she turned to face me. "Gerd's in the damn city, isn't she?"

"The counterspell happened too quickly for her not to be within the walls," I murmured.

"Have you seen anything like this?" Dragonfly gestured at the brilliant pink spot on her table. Gerd's hair had burned far hotter than it should have.

"Yes," I muttered. "Now, I know where Bianca picked up that little trick." Except Bianca's counterspell to prevent me from tracking her cohort Drest through magic didn't have the alien feel of demon power.

"Bianca used demon magic?" Dragonfly's eyes widened, and she dropped to the couch.

Little Bear snorted as he reentered the sitting room. "She tried to kill the chief justice with it, too. She just didn't count on us tracking down her accomplice through old-fashioned logical reasoning."

I sat down on the couch opposite of Dragonfly and compared the two situations. The effect of the counterspell was far more pronounced on Gerd's sample than it had been on Drest's. Was it because Bianca cast the spell on his behalf whereas Gerd cast on her own body detritus?

Or was Gerd further along the path to becoming a skinwalker than Bianca had been?

That seemed the more logical conclusion based on the facts and my observations of demons and the way their magic contaminated objects and people in our plane of existence. But had I just destroyed the lock of Gerd's hair in the possession of the Reverend Mother of Balance? Did it matter if she hadn't bothered to use it? Or had Gerd's ally within the home Temple of Balance already destroyed the lock for her? Was the loss of the lock why the Reverend Mother hadn't tracked Gerd before now?

Too many questions chased through my head like a puppy that chased its own tail.

"What do we try next, Anthea?" Dragonfly murmured.

"Something a little more conventional." I pushed to my feet, only to wobble as if I were drunk at the thrum of magic beneath the high sister's carpet. The taste of unwatered wine filled my mouth. Ben's second must have shut down the Vintner tunnel access. It reminded me of how much I needed to do before I could relax in my own bed.

"Maybe it would be best if you return to Balance, m'lady." Little Bear sounded concerned, but he wouldn't meet my gaze. I couldn't blame him. Not after the way I behaved a few moments ago.

"First, we need to go to Vintner," I stated firmly. "There's something I want to check on before I formally interrogate High Brother Ben and Chief Warden Mangas." I bowed to Dragonfly. "Thank you for your assistance this evening, High Sister."

"I owe Chief Warden Little Bear more for his quick thinking." Dragonfly inclined her head to him. "Otherwise, I would have had far more damage to my Temple than a scorch mark on my rug."

"We're here to serve." Little Bear politely nodded.

"Anthea, before you leave—" Dragonfly shook her head, setting the bells of her robes jingling. "You don't think Ben's a renegade, do you?"

She wanted some hope. That I could understand.

"Mya's initial examination of him says no." I tried to smile, to reassure my fellow priestess. "I will have to do a formal interrogation before I can fully clear him."

She nodded in response.

I took my leave, Little Bear at my side. Both my eyes and nose stung at the smoke from the cold room lingering in the air. A few worshippers argued with Claudia near the entrance of Love, but my appearance deterred any further complaints, and they swiftly departed.

"Sister," I said as we approached her. "It might be best for you and the baby to sleep on the roof tonight with all the smoke in your Temple."

"Yes, m'lady." She laughed, a sweet feminine one that I'd never had. "Luc's right. Chaos seems to follow you everywhere."

"I don't remember having this much trouble until I was assigned to Orrin." But even I had to chuckle despite the twinge of jealousy I felt. "Good eventide, Sister."

"And you, Chief Justice."

As my chief warden and I headed down the boulevard toward the Temple of Vintner, Little Bear asked, "Permission to speak freely, Chief Justice?"

From the rough catch in his throat, I knew what he wanted to address. As much as I wished he would forget the entire incident, I also knew he wasn't one to ignore such a breach of protocol.

"Granted," I choked out.

"What the demon happened to you in Love?" he exclaimed.

"Please keep your voice down," I hissed.

"I understand the edict, but—"

"It had nothing to do with the edit from the home Temples." Magic thrummed through the cobblestones. The cold fury of Conflict. It was followed by the scents of apples, potatoes and maize. Child.

"Then why did you—"

"I'm having trouble controlling my reaction to the magic being performed in Orrin this evening," I blurted.

"The seats shutting down the entrances to the tunnel system?" He sounded skeptical.

"High Sister Mya just destroyed the spell in Child, and now I'm very hungry." My stomach rumbled loud enough the warden guarding the Wildling Temple chuckled as we passed him.

"It could be Justice Yanaba's connection with the city is affecting you," Little Bear suggested.

"It's entirely possible, but the more likely answer is I'm having trouble blocking the essence of every living thing in Orrin," I grumbled. "You and High Brother Luc are right. I'm too close to the problem."

"Having your very own mother wanting you dead would be highly disconcerting for anyone," he said before lowering his voice. "What would be more disconcerting is having your head of household stabbing your chief warden in his sleep because you are indiscriminately kissing people."

"I said I was sorry," I snapped.

"I told you what happened with Chief Warden Maebh of Mother during the Spring Rituals three years ago," he ground out. "Sivan would be even more upset you took liberties—"

"How about we never speak of this again?" Once again, my face burned. "Because if Sivan finds out, she'll slit my throat after she's done with you."

"Agreed," Little Bear said. "Assuming you can keep your libido under control."

I barely reined in my explosion of temper. He had every right to be irritated with my actions, but I didn't appreciate his accusation I had no self-control whatsoever.

"Chief Warden, I hereby rescind permission for you to speak freely for the rest of the night."

"Very well, m'lady," he muttered.

We remained silent the rest of the way to Vintner. The temple had so many lamps burning it was all I could do not to wince. The main doors stood wide open, and the dark quartz statue of Vintner smiling and holding out his arms in welcome was very visible against the backdrop of yellow-white heat. At the top of the Temple's steps, the warden standing guard inclined his head.

"High Brother Luc and Justice Elizabeth are awaiting you in our garden, Chief Justice."

Little Bear grunted at Luc's expectation I would check up on him and Elizabeth. I ignored his disgruntled mood.

"Thank you, Warden." I smiled and charged through the Temple. Vintner was laid out in a similar pattern to Balance. However, its rear courtyard was much, much larger than ours. It was necessary for growing and brewing so many of the medicines our people needed.

Whereas the Healers Guild had a tempestuous relationship with the Temple of Death, Vintner encouraged a close relationship with the guild. So close, Vintner allowed both healers and civilians to study at their home Temple and created a curriculum at the Queen's University. Their goals were the same—the health and well-being of the people. And quite simply, there weren't enough healers. Vintner provided medical training to those without magic talent so isolated towns and villages had some recourse for the sick and injured.

Light balls filled a section of the garden beyond Vintner's back porch, not that I could actually see them. The magic spheres didn't give off heat the way lamps or fires did, but Luc's magic tingled against my skin as did Elizabeth's.

I pushed past the staff of Vintner observing Luc and Elizabeth. One of the Vintner wardens started to put hands toward me. She jerked back, whether it was Little Bear's low-throated, wordless growl or the Vintner warden's recognition of my red eyes.

"Chief Justice." She bowed. A murmur ran through the crowd. Most of their comments regarded my strange appearance, but for once it wasn't about the unusual color of my eyes. I wasn't wearing my standard uniform, and they were surprised I was actually pretty.

Human beings could be so ridiculous at times. In a way, I was glad they all looked the same to me.

Little Bear stayed behind and spoke with the Vintner wardens about getting the staff back inside the Temple. Luc stood propped on his crutches near a corpse. Elizabeth knelt by the corpse's side. Time jerked as she released her rewind.

Have you detected any demon magic? I demanded as I approached.

Thank you for using silent speech, Luc chided. *The clergy and staff of Vintner are shaken up enough.*

But? I prompted.

Yes, Elizabeth said.

My body trembled at the confirmation. This had gone so much further than a woman disgruntled over her illegal conception or her grab for power.

Do you feel up to doing a rewind of Ben's quarters?

Yes, Elizabeth said.

Anything in particular I should be looking for? Luc asked.

Yes, but I don't want to taint your perception of the rewind. I sighed. *We'll compare notes when you are finished here.*

Does your presence here have anything to do with the emergency bells at Love? A layer of humor coated Elizabeth's mental voice.

Yes, I grudgingly admitted. *I was following a lead.*

Luc tried to suppress his smile, but he failed horribly. "We shall report out findings shortly, Chief Justice."

"Thank you, High Brother." I inclined my head to them before I pivoted and marched back through the Temple of Vintner.

As Little Bear and I walked up the boulevard toward Balance, the only horse and wagon on the street was the one from the Healers Guild.

Warden Noko accompanied Master Bly and her apprentice Simi. The three women nodded politely at us as they passed. A few steps later, I felt Wildling and Death closed their passageways.

"When we get back to Balance, would you please send a messenger to Magistrate DiCook?" I murmured to Little Bear.

"He's probably in bed, m'lady."

"I know, but we just trapped a very dangerous animal within the walls of Orrin," I replied. "We're going to need all the help we can get."

Chapter 13

My interrogation of High Brother Ben went as I expected. His anger and grief coated Brother Garbhan's truthspell, but Ben wasn't lying about his memories Mya had unlocked. I was glad for Jax and Talbert's presence in the Balance reception room. Part of me feared what Ben might do to himself when we finished and I told him of Golden Eagle's fate.

I allowed Ben to stay for his chief warden's interrogation. Mangas was totally innocent. However, he was quite perturbed over what had happened to the priest he was responsible for and the loss of one of his wardens. There hadn't been any change to the wardens' duty schedule. It seemed the poor man's death was a result of being in the wrong place at the wrong time.

When we finished, Ben ran his fingers through his hair. Though he wore it unbound and long in the Chumash style, it was very curly. He blamed it on an ancestor from the Levant, a territory on the eastern side of the Middle Sea.

But I could understand his grief after what Gerd's machinations did to Luc and my grandfather Kam.

"Did she cast some kind of demon spell on Warden Golden Eagle, too?" Ben asked softly.

"The preliminary investigation says so," I replied.

"Why?" Ben shook his head. "Golden Eagle wasn't even a passive talent. He was no threat to her."

"She needed a power source for what she plans next." I shrugged. "She would have done the same to whichever Vintner warden was guarding you last night."

My statement struck Ben speechless. Talbert's visage was stolid and unmoved, as if he suspected the truth himself.

However, Jax sputtered with shock and anger. "You can't be serious!"

"Deadly serious." My shoulders sagged as the day's events caught up with me.

At the soft rap on the doors, Little Bear checked who was there, but I felt DiCook's presence before Warden Ailyn knocked to announce his arrival. I quickly told him of the events since . . .

Holy Balance, had it only been the midday meal since I last spoke to Malven? So much had happened. When I came to Golden Eagle's forced suicide, the magistrate's mein shifted to the same stony expectation Talbert's had.

"Getting herself trapped within the city walls may be part of Gerd's plan." DiCook stroked his beard.

"That is also what I fear, but to what end?" I murmured.

"Anthea, you said you wanted my opinion on something," Talbert said. "And that was before chaos erupted during the convocation."

"Yes." I rose. "Pardon me for a moment, good sirs." I strode out of the reception room and straight to my office. It only took a moment to retrieve the strange coin from the safe hole in the wall. I nearly tripped over Ailyn in my dash out of my office.

"I-I'm so sorry, Chief Justice," the young warden mumbled. Her color turned scarlet, no doubt in her fear I'd reprimand her.

I inhaled to calm my own annoyance. My chief warden was already cross with me this evening. And seeing Ailyn always sent a pang of guilt through me. She replaced Tyra, who had given her life to save me from a demon during the Fall of Tandor.

"I know you are still getting used to guarding a sighted justice." I smiled. "May I suggest keeping an extra pace away so neither of us are covered in unintentional bruises?"

"Of course, Chief Justice," she stammered.

But she listened as we jogged back to the reception room. Maybe there was some hope for her. By the time we returned, Luc, Elizabeth, and their wardens had come back from Vintner.

"Well?" I looked at Luc.

He sat heavily on a free chair before he spoke. "Ben's quarters are tainted with demon magic. A few personal objects had spells laid on them, and we salted them. We think we found them all, but we want to wait two days before we check again."

Ben crossed his arms. "What about the guest quarters and the wardens' barracks?"

"Everything else was clean." Elizabeth sat on the chair to which Gina had guided her. "I don't suppose I can get some wine after doing two rewinds back to back."

"Yes, m'lady." Gina immediately pivoted toward the doors.

"Would you please bring some back for all of us, Warden?" I asked. My stomach rumbled again. I wanted to flee to my own bedchambers.

Luc laughed out loud. Everyone else managed to keep their reactions to smiles and smirks.

"Yes, m'lady," Gina said cheerfully over her shoulder. "I'll bring some snacks, too." She left the reception room.

I handed the silk covered coin to Talbert before I resumed my seat. He unwrapped the pewter.

The magistrate leaned over Talbert's arm and took a look at the object. DiCook spat out a colorful Cantan oath.

Talbert passed the coin to Jax who sniffed it and shook his head. Jax passed it to Ben.

The high brother held the pewter up to a nearby lamp before he turned back to me. "What the demon is this? And what does it have to do with Gerd?"

Chapter 14

I waited for the high brother of Thief to say something.

Anything.

Talbert pursed his lips before he looked at me. "This merely confirms the Assassins Guild isn't simply working for the renegades. Was this found in Love this morning?"

"No." I shook my head. "Gerd gave the coin to the daughter of the proprietor of the Green Lady Inn after she discovered the secret entrance from the inn to Love had been bricked up by the sisters."

"Are you sure it was Gerd?" Talbert asked.

"According to the girl, she looked a great deal like me but with a smaller nose, curly hair, and normal colored eyes," I replied.

"But the coin is worthless." Ben frowned as he passed it to Mangas. "Why did the girl accept it?"

"She was told to donate it to a Temple." I looked at Talbert. "The innkeeper Alo said he and his daughter attend First Day services at Thief."

He nodded slowly. "Most of the innkeepers in the city do. Another warning. So why didn't the child place it in the offering box?"

"Instinct. I think she has talent," I said. "She could see through Gerd's glamour."

"This is the girl you want me to test?" Luc asked.

"Yes." I nodded.

"What makes you think Gerd wore a glamour?" Talbert asked.

"Because no one recognized Gerd walking through the city three days ago." I shrugged. "According to the girl, Gerd hadn't bothered to change her hair or face in any way. She was at the inn on Sixth Day, dressed as a guardswoman with a green oiled cloak—"

"Because it was raining that day," Talbert finished. He pursed his lips and rubbed his chin. "I'll see what I can learn for you, m'lady."

Jax yanked on his wild hair. It was short, but it stood out at various angles. I rather suspected it was because of his second form, but it would be rude for me to ask.

"The only scent any of my people have detected were in the tunnels leading to Love and heading northeast toward Pana Valley," he said. "It led overland to Redwood Grove, which is on this side of the Trill River. The trail seemed to stop at the edge of the city. None of them have picked up the scent anywhere on the opposite bank."

"You should recall anyone who's still searching." I grimaced. "I don't want them caught in a renegade ambush. Gerd is definitely in the city."

"How can you be sure?" Ben asked.

"Because I nearly burned down Love by accident while performing a tracking spell to find her."

"Was it like the counterspell when we tried to track Drest last month?" Elizabeth asked.

"Yes, but it was magnitudes more powerful, faster, and this time, it had a demon flavor to it," I answered.

"That is why you believe Gerd to be nearby?" Elizabeth said. "Have you considered the possibility a demon is wearing her skin?"

"If she were dead, the tracking spell wouldn't have worked, and there wouldn't be the need for a counterspell." Luc grinned. "Unfortunately, we had too much experience with the variety of techniques demons use in Tandor."

"That is what I fear, High Brother," Elizabeth said mournfully. "That the demons will or have discovered a way to keep the skin alive while they wear it. Just like they do with their skins that bind their grimoires."

Thankfully, Gina, Sivan, and the housekeeping ladies arrived with pitchers and platters. They were followed by Ming Wei guiding Yanaba into the room.

My junior justice smiled in my general direction. "So, I hear we have a demon dealer running around Orrin. And here, I feared we would have a boring midsummer."

Once DiCook learned about what we did to the Temple entrances to the tunnel system, he volunteered to go to the Mining Guild and arrange to close up the three exits beyond the city walls. One of his cousins was the chief of the guild, and he owed DiCook a few favors.

Everyone but Luc left shortly after we developed a tentative plan for the Temples to assist Orrin's peacekeepers in watching the three city gates. This time, we would need clergy on the gates, not just wardens. Some of the priests and priestesses would believe such a duty beneath them.

Luc sent his chief warden Nicholas back to Light. Xander arrived a moment after Nicholas left, and he and Yanaba retired to her bedchamber for the night. Elizabeth chuckled quietly to herself before she said good night as well. Gina guided the justice back to her room.

Ailyn and Luc followed me to my bedroom. I held up my hand when the warden tried to follow us inside.

"Justice Yanaba sealed the passageway," I said gently. "You no longer have to stay in my room with me."

"Oh." Ailyn's cheeks blazed crimson. "Um, I will stand guard out here then. Good eventide, Chief Justice."

I closed and locked my bedchamber door before I warded the room. Not that I distrusted Ailyn, but she didn't need to overhear some things.

"You should still keep a warden in here," Luc murmured.

"So Gerd can force them to hang themselves when she gets in here?" I couldn't stop my bitterness from spilling out while I removed my sword and harness.

"If she gets in here," Luc amended. "Little Bear won't let that happen."

It was a good thing Luc couldn't see my face since my own skin burned. Why in all the names of the Twelve had I kissed my chief warden? We had created a good working relationship over the last year, and I managed to ruin it in an instant of uncontrolled emotion.

Damn, why couldn't I have kissed Dragonfly instead? She would have laughed about it, and I would have endured some teasing over the next few months, but it wouldn't have mattered so much.

I could understand Little Bear's concern over Sivan learning about the incident. My concerns were even greater. I needed Sivan to run this damn Temple. I couldn't afford to lose her.

She wasn't the only one with a jealous streak. Luc had been very irate with Ambassador Quan's attempts to woo me, even though nothing had happened between us. Nor would it ever. But Luc had no right to accuse me of such things when he'd been ordered to breed a child with a priestess. Any fertile priestess.

Is that why I kissed Little Bear? Some part of me wanted revenge because Luc slept with Claudia? Balance, if that were true, I was being incredibly pathetic. Ironically, Sivan would have been the person I would have talked to about this problem. Or rather, she would have nagged me until I did.

"According to Shi Hua, Ambassador Quan has ordered more ingredients for flash powder," Luc said.

It took a moment for my thoughts to shift to a new topic.

"Anthea?" he said.

"Ingredients?" I started yanking the numerous pins from my hair. "I thought the ingredients for flash powder could only be found in Jing."

"Apparently not." He grinned as he loosened the ties of his tunic.

"This is not supposed to go beyond the two of us. The story will be he imported it from Jing. However, he's located sources within Issura and the Plains Nations."

"It sounds like he was busier in Tandor than I realized." I yanked more pins and tossed them on my desk. For the love of Balance, how many of the blasted things had Sivan stuck in my hair?

"Come here before you irrevocably tangle your hair, and we have to shave it off." Luc sat on my bed and patted the space between his thighs.

"I didn't want such a complicated style. Shaving it all off would be so much cooler in this summer's heat," I grumbled, but I sat down as he suggested. His fingers gently plucked the pins from my tresses.

"You looked very nice though," he murmured.

"You're just saying that," I grumbled some more. I liked his compliment more than I wanted to admit.

"Everyone was surprised by your appearance tonight," he continued.

I grimaced at his words. "Chumana already pointed out my nose is much larger than Gerd's."

"The innkeeper's daughter?" Luc chuckled. "Did she point out your heart is much larger than Gerd's as well?" He set the pins on the lampstand by my bed and picked up my brush. His gestures as he dealt with the tangles I'd caused reminded me of the nights on circuit when he would comb out my hair by the fire.

"If we'd run away to Cant after I executed Samael DiRoy, we wouldn't be caught up in her revenge scheme," I said softly.

"And Gerd would have taken over Orrin, she and Bianca would still be selling children, and everyone in our Temples would have been hung for Gerd's corrupt magic," he growled. "Is that what you truly would want? Young Nathan swinging from the end of a rope?"

"No!" I snapped. "Of course not! I—" I closed my eyes against the burning sensation that had nothing to do with the smoke from the fires at Love.

Luc set my brush aside and wrapped his arms around my midriff, pulling my back tight against his chest. "Talk to me, my love."

"I-I—" I swallowed hard to get the lump out of my throat. "I'm overwhelmed. We should be dealing with the every day minutiae of Orrin's legal work, not wrapped up in mad people trying to end the existence of the human race by feeding us to demons."

The only sound was our breathing. Luc's heartbeat and mine meshed. I could have stayed in this little moment of peace forever.

"If we had gone to Cant, the demons would have already killed us," he murmured against my skin. "As much as we both hate what is happening now, the Twelve made sure we were where we needed to be."

I sighed. "Do you really think they have a plan? Because right now, I feel certain all Twelve of Them are making everything up as they go."

He chuckled and kissed my shoulder. "You should be whipped for such blasphemy."

"Oh, really?" I looked over my shoulder at him. "And who's going to punish me? You?"

"Possibly." He kissed me. I knew he was merely trying to get me out of my maudlin mood, and I was perfectly willing to let him.

Chapter 15

The next morning, three loud *BOOM*s woke the rest of the city. Luc looked up and grinned at me. "Guess the Miners Guild are getting a head start on their day."

"Shut up and finish your own task," I said.

"I'd never leave a lady justice unsatisfied," he said in mock dismay. He finished what he started, which he did quite well.

After he left for his Temple duties and I drank my first pot of tea, I summoned my squire Nathan to my office. "How are things going with your friends Cat and Dog?" The two children were the unofficial leaders of Orrin's street orphans. I found it was helpful to cultivate my own sources of information in the city, instead of relying on Thief. It helped my squire had been one of their members until he had been caught stealing bread last winter.

Nathan cocked his head. "What do you want them to do, Lady Justice?"

"I see we're getting right to the point this morning." I tried hard not to grin.

"The older ones aren't going to waste time with the social niceties. They're like you. Cut to the chase and say what you want."

"You are totally correct, Squire. Do you think they might be willing to help me track down a wanted fugitive like they helped me with finding Drest?"

"For a price," Nathan said bluntly. But I expected no less.

"Very well. Are they getting enough to eat?" I asked. My staff's food and blanket donations to the street children had been one of the many contentions between High Mother Leocadia and myself. She blamed me for the orphans not accepting shelter at her Temple, but it would take a long time before the street children trusted the Temples again after what Bianca and Drest had done to them.

If they ever did. Many of them questioned Nathan's honesty about how he and Ming Wei were treated at Balance.

Nathan squirmed a bit before he blurted, "Yes. Everyone on the south side knows Sivan and Hogarth are Temple, so High Brother Jax, Sister Farrah, or Brother Sisquoc have been coming with me to the south side. The mothers next door don't pay no mind to me coming and going. And the other kids don't realize the animals with me are Temple."

I sat back in my chair. I wasn't sure which surprised me more, my squire's ingenuity for getting food to the orphans or how he managed to finagle assistance from the Wildlings.

"How do you explain the animals then?"

Nathan grinned. "They wear a jeweled collar and a leash. I tell the others you lend me out to Ambassador Quan, and I walk his pets. I tell them I filch the food from the ambassador."

I put my face in my hands, unsure of whether to be appalled at what Nathan was doing or to find this course of action very humorous. The humor won out, and I started laughing.

"I'm glad you're still helping them." I smiled at Nathan. "How soon can I meet with Cat and Dog?"

"I already took a load down this week." His mouth twisted as he considered the issue. "Leaving a message with Govind would be the fastest way."

"Govind?" My skin tightened as my eyebrows rose. "The Tandoran silversmith?"

Nathan nodded. "His shop is one of our meeting places. He pays them to watch it and to help him with tasks. Dog's hoping Govind might take him on as an apprentice next year."

Once again, I was surprised, not only by Nathan's ingenuity, but Govind's willingness to help when he had his own family to support. He and his business partner, a blacksmith, were already receiving stipends from both Balance and Thief for the items we needed.

"Have you broken your fast?" I asked.

He nodded.

I handed him a silver. "That's for Govind for relaying the message. You'd better get going so you don't miss them."

Nathan rose and rushed to the office door.

"And make sure you tell Hogarth you're running an errand for me before you disappear."

"Yes, m'lady!" My squire bobbed his head before he dashed through the doorway.

Of course, Cat and Dog showed up at our postern gate in time for the midday meal.

Sivan set a private table in the Balance reception room for our guests, our squires, and the three justices. Neither Little Bear nor Gina were happy I banned any wardens from attending, but I knew I would get more information from the children without guards. As far as the street urchins were concerned, wardens were the same as peacekeepers.

But first came the negotiations once we were seated around the table.

"How much you willing to pay?" Cat said with a lift of her chin. Dog let her handle the bargaining while he dug into his plateful of roasted chicken, corn pudding, and fresh blackberries.

"The same as last time," I said "One silver."

"Except I don't know how many questions you'll ask this time." She considered for a moment before she said, "A copper a question."

"Deal." I removed a bag of coins from my cloak pocket and set it next to my plate. "I'm looking for Gerd, the former high sister of Love. Have you seen her?"

A sharp bark of laughter came from Dog. "Even we know the sisters of Love gotta wear veils in public. Those things may be finely woven, but the whole point is to hide their faces. How are we supposed to know what she looks like?"

"Well, you can't fault the boy's logic, Anthea." Elizabeth grinned in my direction.

"And it's not our fault if you ask stupid questions either, Lady Justice." Cat motioned with her forefinger for a copper. I drew one from the bag and slid it across the table to her.

"Point taken. Let's try another tactic." I leaned my elbows on the table. "Have you seen a woman who looks like me, but with a smaller nose and brown eyes? She may have been dressed as a guardswoman and wearing a green oiled cloak with a hood when it rains."

Dog elbowed his partner. "Told you that wasn't the Red Justice in disguise."

The other three children stared at him in horror. Even Elizabeth and Yanaba stared in the direction of his voice.

"Say you're sorry," Cat hissed.

"I've been called worse, Cat." I turned to Dog. "Though it is unwise to insult your hostess at the dinner table, good sir."

Dog gulped and wiped chicken grease off his fingers and onto his tunic before he bowed his head and said, "I'm sorry, Chief Justice."

"I like you, Dog. I don't want you getting yourself knifed by accidentally disrespecting someone," I said. "However, thank you for the apology."

"We did see someone who looked very similar to you, but it was her bearing that caught our attention," Cat said. "She didn't walk like any guardswoman I've ever seen." The girl pursed her lips before she said, "She was confident, but not in the way of someone who works for a living. More like the duke's sister."

I frowned and slid two more coppers to Cat. "Lady Alessa?"

Dog's mouth was full, so he nodded in agreement while chewing furiously.

"If I may, Chief Justice?" Ming Wei piped up. The girl rarely spoke, except to Nathan and Yanaba.

"Please, Squire." I gestured for her to continue.

She hopped off her chair because she was rather small for her age. "The nobles and most of the priestesses walk like this." She walked in a familiar gliding stride.

"I take it I'm not as graceful." I set my chin on my hand and smiled.

Ming Wei shook her head. "You walk more like the sisters of Wildling and Conflict or a warden. You know how to fight so your stance is constantly ready for battle. It's why most people are afraid of you."

"And how do I walk, my dear squire?" Yanaba teased.

"That's different. You and Justice Elizabeth have to walk carefully because you don't want to hurt yourselves." Ming Wei resumed her seat at the table. "But you both still walk like you expect a fight."

Elizabeth sighed. "I fear in both of our cases, it's due to experience."

I reached into my bag and pushed two more coppers to Cat. "So I walk more like a real guardswoman than the woman you saw?"

"Yes, m'lady."

I pushed another copper to her. "Do you know where she's staying?"

"No, but we could find out for that silver." Cat grinned at me.

"If you can, I would be grateful. But—" I started. When Cat opened her mouth, I held up my right forefinger. At her silence, I continued, "You, Dog, and the other street children cannot take any unnecessary chances. Gerd is far more dangerous than Drest ever was."

Cat's eyes narrowed. "Isn't she your mother?"

"Yes, Cat, she is." I leaned back in my chair. "And I've lost count of how many times she's tried to kill me."

Chapter 16

After the midday meal, I gave Cat and Dog five more coppers each for their time and told them to leave any messages with Govind. Once they left, and Nathan and Ming Wei joined Sivan for their reading and writing lessons, my sister justices and I discussed the situation over a decanter of chilled wine.

"You shouldn't be endangering those children," Elizabeth chided.

"Can you think of a different way to find Gerd before she does whatever she's planning?" I snapped. "Beatrice brought down an entire demon army by killing herself. Can you even conceive of the chaos and destruction Gerd would cause with energy from the people she's murdered so far?"

"That's the problem, Anthea," Yanaba said softly. "Can you imagine what she would do to any of the street children if she catches them spying on her?"

"Unfortunately, I can." I closed my eyes and clenched my fists. "I saw what was done to Yellow Fin, Gregorios, and Golden Eagle. Gerd can and will do far, far worse."

"You're letting your personal feelings toward her cloud your judgment," Elizabeth stated. "When it puts innocent lives at risk, we have to say something."

I opened my eyes and stared at her. However, the effect of my red orbs was lost on a blind woman.

"Do you even understand what her goal is?" I hissed. "It's always the same. If she can't control something, bend it to her own use, then she will destroy it. That's what she plans to do to Orrin!" I smacked the palms of my hands against the table top, making the other two justices jump.

"The sheer fact Nathan's friends recognized her means she probably isn't using a glamour when she's in the south side, assuming she is at all," Yanaba mused. She was deliberately changing the subject, for which I was grateful. I hated that everyone seemed to think I had emotional problems in regards to Gerd rather than taking a good look at her pattern of manipulation and power games.

"Considering a good chunk of the population have worshipped with her at one time or another, why wouldn't anyone else recognize her if she weren't using a glamour?" I asked.

Yanaba giggled, and even Elizabeth laughed out loud.

"Because, Chief Justice, they aren't paying attention to Gerd's face when they lay with her," Elizabeth said while wiping the tears from her face.

My skin heated at their implication I was more blind than they were. But then, I saw differently than other sighted people. I enjoyed watching the shift of colors of Luc's skin when we—

I cleared my throat. "So you're saying I shouldn't have Chumana tested?"

"No." Elizabeth waved her hand dismissively. "By all means, have the child tested. My worry is—" She sighed. "I worry that you might be missing obvious clues that could lead us to Gerd with your obsession over demon magic."

"Are you saying you didn't detect demon magic acting upon Golden Eagle?"

"No, that's not what I'm saying," she said crossly.

"Anthea, may we speak as friends and not colleagues for a moment?" Yanaba said softly.

"Yes," I replied though I feared she would be as blunt as Little Bear had been last night.

"I'm concerned you are focusing your anger over the situation between Luc and Claudia towards Gerd."

"I am not—"

Yanaba held up her palms to stop me. "I'm not saying you aren't justified. It is Gerd's fault you cannot conceive, and you have every right to feel the way you do. But I agree with Elizabeth. Your anger is clouding your judgment in these murders."

They were both right on one count. I didn't detect the corner they were backing me into until I was trapped.

"Are you telling me to stand down from my post?" I growled.

Which they could do legally. If two or more justices believed another justice could not objectively perform her duties, she could be told to take leave, pending an investigation by the home Temple.

"Not at this point, Anthea," Elizabeth said. "We're asking you not to push us into making that decision. Using children to spy for you does not help your case."

"Well, it's not like Yanaba didn't say up front she was ordered to spy for the old biddy." I pushed my chair back and stood. "Is there any other warnings you two would like to deliver before I take my leave?"

Yanaba and Elizabeth remained silent. I dropped my wards on the reception room and stalked out.

How the demon had everything gone so wrong in my life?

Chapter 17

There was no sense being political or cagey with my requests to the Reverend Mother for information anymore. I spent the afternoon drafting a letter demanding answers, including why she hadn't used a tracking spell on the lock of Gerd's hair she'd confiscated from me. The Temple bells rang Third Afternoon by the time I finished stamping and proofing the letter.

I sealed it with wax and pressed my personal die into the dark pink puddle. Despite my irritation with Elizabeth and Yanaba's not so subtle threat to unseat me, I didn't want the Reverend Mother's wrath falling on them.

I had barely stood up and stretched when someone pounded on my office door.

"Come in," I yelled.

Gina burst in, her color leaning toward a bright orange. "Sister Claudia is missing."

My warden filled me in as we saddled horses. If we were going to be running all over the damn city, we would need steeds for better time.

"Sister Claudia reported abdominal pains to the high sister around Second Afternoon," Gina said. "Given the sister's only midway through her term, the high sister ordered Warden Jocasta to take the sister straight to the Healers Guild."

"So Jocasta's missing, too?" I asked. Nassa whickered as I mounted her, picking up on the worry and fear coursing through my veins.

"It's like they both vanished." Gina stepped into the left stirrup of her horse and slung herself into the saddle. "High Sister Dragonfly sent out two more wardens when the guild didn't send a runner back with a status after two candlemarks. That's when they discovered Sister Claudia and Jocasta never arrived."

I muttered an obscenity under my breath. I may be upset over the circumstances of Claudia's pregnancy, but I never wanted harm to come to her. But given that anyone with Light talent was a target of the renegades and the demons, we needed to find Claudia and quickly. It was troubling anyone would simply disappear during one of the busiest times of the day in the city.

When we arrived at Love, we weren't the only ones there. Luc sat at a small wooden table in the entryway, surrounded by clergy and wardens. Brother Garbhan stood by Luc's left shoulder. Luc had a large piece of parchment laid out on the table, probably a map from the way he pointed at invisible things on the parchment.

"Warden Jocasta took the back streets to avoid the heavier traffic, but to the best of our knowledge, the wagon never crossed Queen's Gate Street. The magistrate and the peacekeepers are doing a building-to-building sweep in our direction." Luc traced a line with his finger. "The Wildlings and their wardens will head north from here first and try to pick up their scents."

A low rumble went through the assembly. Luc held up his hands. "I know, I know. The odds aren't good, but, Sister Farrah, if you and your people head back to the Love stables, their stablemistress can talk you through Warden Jocasta's initial planned route."

Farrah nodded, but for once, her narrow face didn't carry its usual delight at the world. She and three of the Wildlings turned toward the inner doors. She caught my attention and grimaced.

I stepped closer to her, and she paused. "Where's Jax?" I whispered.

"He and the others are with DiCook." Farrah grabbed my arm. *This is not good. It's been too long on a day that's too busy.* She released me and headed into the Temple, the rest of the Wildling clergy stripping off their clothing as they followed her.

Luc continued issuing orders. ". . . Temple personnel will do the same from the south heading north toward Queen's Gate Street."

"What if the wagon went south for whatever reason?" one of the Conflict sisters asked.

"That's the reason half of you will wait here while the chief justice and I search Sister Claudia's quarters and perform a tracking spell," he replied.

Shouldn't we do the tracking spell first? I asked him at the same time the Conflict sister said the same thing out loud.

"Time is of the essence." Luc looked the sister squarely in the eye. "If Gerd is behind Sister Claudia's disappearance, she's using demon magic, and demon magic can disrupt a tracking spell."

"Which is why Thief and Wildling became the Temple's eyes, ears, and nose," Sister Cedar Grove said.

The Conflict sister bowed her head. "I am here to serve."

"Sister Shi Hua will act as coordinator once we've dispersed." Luc eyed me. "Justice Yanaba?"

"Searching as we speak," I said. "She'll let us know if she finds Sister Claudia."

Sister Cedar Grove frowned. "I know Justice Yanaba is bound to Orrin, but can she sort through thousands of people?"

"Therein lies the problem," Luc said. "It'll take time for the justice to search through the population, and time is not a luxury we have. Sister Farrah and the Wildlings are on their way. Those of you assigned to follow them—" He waved toward the side street, running between Love and Wildling.

The Conflict sister who'd questioned Luc and half the group headed down the steps and around the corner. I realized why the Wildlings went through the Temple itself—they needed a fresh sample of Claudia and Jocasta's scents from their personal effects.

Luc grabbed his crutches and lurched to his foot. "Light wardens, stay out here for the time being."

Chief Warden Nicolas opened his mouth to protest, but before he could say a word, Gina said, "I swear upon my life I'll guard Light and Balance."

"The more important task, Warden, is not letting the chief justice start another fire," Sister Raven Claw said with a smile.

"Chief Warden Little Bear warned me to get a bucket of water before she does another tracking spell." Gina grinned.

As the three of us entered the Temple, I muttered, "Does everyone know about how the damn fire started?"

Gina shrugged. "It's not often one of the Temples rings the fire code. It was a major subject of discussion at the market this afternoon from what Sivan said."

Luc didn't even have to ask where Claudia's quarters were. I already wanted to curl up in a ball with the covers over my head as I did when I was a child over the market gossip about me. Seeing the bed where they lay ripped at my heart.

Claudia's bedchambers were smaller than the high sister's. More functional than seductive. The only real differences between my quarters and hers were the high window that let in light and air, the mirrored dressing table with a myriad of cosmetics, and the two crossed fishing spears and netting above her bed. Curious her choice in weapons, but then I'd seen her in action with only her hairpins and nails during the battle to retake the Temple of Love from the renegades last winter. She could fight just as viciously as any priestess from Conflict.

"How can we do this without setting Claudia's entire room on fire?" I asked.

"If my tracking spell is hijacked like yours was, I want you to time freeze the room," Luc said.

"Are you two mad?"

It wasn't Gina's voice behind me. I turned around. Dragonfly stood in the doorway, her veil flung back over her head so I could see her scowl. One of the new Love wardens peered around her arm. The warden had more of a concerned expression.

"No." Luc shook his head. "It's the safest way to find Claudia without letting any renegade sorcerer, including Gerd, destroy your Temple."

Dragonfly cocked her head. "This is a working Temple, High Brother. Claudia's hair, the smallest chips from her nails, flakes of skin even, will be all over this facility no matter how diligently my staff cleans the place." She turned her scowl on me. "Your tracking spell not only damaged our cold room. It also scorched quite a few possessions of Sister Zinha's, including a tapestry her grandmothers wove for her when she became a novice."

I winced. "I owe her amends."

"Excuse me, but why would Sister Zihna be in Gerd's old quarters?" Luc gestured with both hands. "I thought you were in the high sister's suite."

"I have been in the suite since Gerd was appointed high sister, as was her former second Sister Ilina." Dragonfly's expression turned sour. "Gerd was too lazy to want to deal with the worshippers who came through the tunnel system." She shrugged. "The other bedchamber is slightly bigger than the formal high sister suite. Claudia had first right of refusal as my second, but she didn't want them. Said there was too much bad juju. So as third in seniority, Zihna accepted them."

"Juju?" I frowned.

"It's a term from the western side of the Cradle for imbalance." Dragonfly grimaced. "Maybe we need to cleanse the entire damn Temple."

"Do you have a better idea?" Luc said quietly. His anguish scraped against my own psyche. He blamed himself for Claudia's disappearance because she carried his child.

Except everything came back to my mother's hatred of me. She wouldn't have touched Claudia if she weren't carrying Luc's child. And she wouldn't have touched Luc if not for me. She saw the truth of our feelings for each other though we managed to hide it from everyone else for the longest of times.

"Dragonfly, it's our best chance of finding Claudia and Jocasta," I murmured. "I'll do my best not to hurt anyone else in the process."

The high sister of Love sucked in a deep breath. "Can you freeze the entire building? Just in case."

"I can, but that means I'd be putting out the fires by myself." I frowned as I thought about it. "Can we fill buckets before hand?"

"That will take time." Luc's brows made a green arrowhead between his eyes.

Anthea? Yanaba's presence tickled the back of my mind. *What if we just freeze the counterspell if it attacks the tracking spell?*

"How do we separate the two?" I asked both aloud and silently. Luc joined the link so he could Hear my junior justice.

Place the pieces of Claudia you use in a metal box or canister, Yanaba said. *You keep time running on the tracking spell. I'll freeze the rest of the Temple of Love.*

"Why in the Twelve do you think that will work?" I said.

Because you've been the one running around the city like a crazy person, which gives Elizabeth and me time to experiment. Yanaba's laughter tinkled like the bells on the robes of Love's clergy.

Well, Twelve take me. I looked at Luc.

He shrugged. "We have nothing to lose at this point."

I looked up at Dragonfly.

"Do it." She closed her eyes. "The staff is filling up baths and buckets.

Sister Cedar Grove has moved the others out of the foyer and onto the street."

I dashed into Claudia's small bathing room, stopped the pool, and turned on the cold water spigot. I located a jar of salt on her shelves and poured some in the pool before I returned to the bedchamber. I wouldn't have to worry about the pool overflowing. Yanaba's spell would stop it from filling momentarily.

A few heartbeats later, Dragonfly opened her eyes and nodded. "We're ready."

I grabbed a ceramic mixing dish and a brush from Claudia's dressing table and dragged the stool over to Luc with the toe of my boot. Tension filled the room as I set the dish on the stool and added a few strands of Claudia's hair. When I replaced the brush, I shoved the cosmetic jars to one side of their silver tray and set the brush next to them.

"We need a box to put the dish in." Luc pointed at the altar in the corner. "What about that stone prayer box?"

I carefully removed the ruby heart, the silver bell, and the incense sticks from the soapstone box. Love magic tickled my skin from the items. I hoped Claudia would forgive me for touching her personal religious tools.

The cosmetic dish just barely fit in the bottom of the box, but I'd rather have to replace the dish than the beautifully carved soapstone. Some of the carving edges were worn with use. Therefore, this was a family heirloom or a gift from another sister. I didn't want it to crack from the extreme heat of the counterspell if our idea failed.

I took a step back. The eerie feeling of Yanaba watching through my eyes was a bit disconcerting as Luc started the tracking spell. A ribbon of energy formed from Claudia's hair. Everything seemed to occur as it should when the room froze.

Chapter 18

Yanaba? I said silently.

I still hear you. Her concentration shifted, but to what, I didn't know. *The counterspell has started. I'm trying to backtrack the source.*

Elizabeth drifted into our link, supporting and enforcing Yanaba's efforts. *A least we know Claudia is still alive.*

For now. I couldn't think about what might be happening to the poor priestess. If I did, I'd go mad myself.

Anthea, can you release the tracking spell? Yanaba asked.

I made a child's good luck gesture, hoping Thief would grant me this one small mercy. Concentrating, I carved a small hole inside Claudia's soapstone box and allowed time to continue forward.

I held my breath, half-expecting my spell would collapse Yanaba's spell over the Temple. However, it didn't. Luc's tracking spell extended, fed by my own energy. *It's headed down to the warehouse district.* I focused a bit more. *The DiRoma warehouse. The same one Drest and his cronies were using.*

That's where I'm detecting the source of the counterspell, Yanaba said grimly. *But there's an additional problem. If we don't let both spells complete—*

The renegades will know we've discovered their location. I considered the problem. *When you restart time, can you slow it enough for me to put out the fires? We can't destroy an entire Temple and kill everyone inside in order to catch these traitors.*

Are you mad? Elizabeth said at the same time Yanaba said, *Yes.*

After a heartbeat, Yanaba added, *It'll be easier for me to slow down the passage of time because of my link to the city.*

I'm ready when you are, I replied.

The first discordant beat of the counterspell vibrated through every atom of my being. The strands of Claudia's hair blazed white, forcing me to squint when I snatched up the soapstone box. I ran back into the bath and dumped the box and its contents into the pool.

I continued racing back and forth with any of her belongings that flared from the counterspell. Her brush. Her comb. Her spare set of maternity robes. I was out of breath by the time I ducked under Dragonfly's arm and into the corridor.

The rest of the Temple was easier to deal with since Claudia remained on the first floor, and she was no longer worshipping with the devout. Not to mention, all the sisters of Love were tyrants when it came to cleanliness. I dumped water on all the flares I could find even the one little one in a private worshipping room where one of Claudia's long curling hairs had become entangled with the fibers of a rug. The hair was probably the same color as the yarn which was why it had been missed.

All right, Yanaba. I looked around Love's main receiving room. *I think I've soaked all the potential fires.*

Time inside the Temple snapped back to now. Splashing was followed by cries of shock and dismay from several suddenly drenched staff and clergy. Luckily, it wasn't the Temple's normal worshipping hours.

I ran back to Claudia's quarters. Dragonfly was just coming out of the bathing room when I charged through the doorway.

"Well?" Gina said. She looked at me expectantly as did Luc and Dragonfly.

I grinned though my expression probably looked incredibly vicious. "We have a location."

Yellow-hot smoke billowed from the warehouse district as we approached. We all spurred our horses into a gallop. Thank the Twelve, shipping wasn't at its normal levels this summer.

Peacekeepers, sailors, and dockworkers had already formed lines to aim hoses at the burning DiRoma warehouse. Others manned the pumps that sent seawater into the flames.

DiCook's lieutenant Jaime led the efforts. When he saw me, he ran up to Nassa. I patted her neck, and a flicker of calming magic kept my startled horse from attacking the peacekeeper.

"Is there anything you can do, Chief Justice?" he shouted over the mayhem.

Heat and humid air rolled over us. I tried to take in the insanity. The lower half of the building's walls were brick. However, the rest was wood, and it was fully engulfed by the fire. From the pink and red edging the nearby roofs, the closest buildings were about to burst into flames as well.

"Have your people stop the hoses for a moment," I shouted over the roaring and snapping of the burning warehouse. "When the flames freeze in place, start up the pumps again."

Sister Cedar Grove was by my side as I approached as close as I dared to go.

"Retreat!" I ordered.

"No!" she shouted back. "If I mist some of the water pumped into the building, it'll limit air and douse the flames faster."

Her plan was a sound one, and I nodded.

"Ready?"

"Yes!"

I reached out with my hands and murmured the words to my spell.

Ironically, a freeze spell was a little easier than a rewind, but the energy expenditure was still massive. And the larger the physical space a justice froze, the energy cost rose exponentially.

In the back of my mind, Yanaba and Elizabeth fed me what strength they had left, but it wasn't much after they'd frozen the entire Temple of Love moments ago.

The sudden silence deafened me for an instant before Jaime howled, "Now!"

Water gushed from hoses as the people who manned the pumps sang some sea shanty to keep in rhythm. Like inside Love, the water stopped on the gently sloped roof, caught in my spell. The roof would probably collapse with the weight of the water gathering on it, but it would save the nearby buildings. Above my spell, Cedar Grove shifted some of the water into a heavy mist that would inundate the warehouse.

"Everyone get back!"

Jaime passed the order and the people manning the pumps and hoses retreated.

"Three, two, one!" I released the time freeze spell. A couple of cracks and groans came from the support beam before they collapsed under the weight of the seawater. Cedar Grove's mist boiled down and out before rising again. The burning timbers hissed like a giant bed of snakes.

I couldn't see a damn thing in the greenish-yellow combination of smoke and fog that rolled over us. It felt like we'd turned Orrin into a giant steam room, like those in the public bath houses, but it burned my eyes and stung my nose. Coughing echoed oddly through the haze. However, when the fog and smoke dissipated, the flames were extinguished.

A ragged cheer went up from the people fighting the fire. I looked around the crowd. The clergy and wardens accompanying me had assisted with a couple of extra hoses and pumps.

Cedar Grove laughed and clapped my right shoulder. "We look like a couple of drowned rats, but your crazy idea worked."

"As did yours." I frowned. "But were Sister Claudia and Warden Jocasta in there?"

Cedar Grove muttered an obscenity under her breath.

Peacekeeper Jaime joined us. "We'll need to let the embers cool before we can check the interior." He shook his head. "We're damn lucky the fire was near enough to the bay we could use the seawater to put it out."

Exhaustion plucked at my muscles. I wanted nothing more than to curl up in my bed and sleep for a week, but we still had to find Gerd and the missing Love women. Some instinct said this was a distraction from whatever she planned. "High Brother Luc, relay a message to High Sister Dragonfly."

He didn't answer me aloud or silently.

I whirled around, searching for him.

Luc's wardens Nicholas and Tadhg ran up to me.

"He ordered us to assist with fighting the blaze." Chief Warden Nicholas looked around. His growing wave of horror beat against my mind.

"His horse is still there." Tadhg pointed at the hitching posts down the cross street where all of us left our mounts.

Gina ran up to me. "What's going on?"

"Have you seen High Brother Luc?" I asked.

"He stayed with the horses . . ." The expression on her face when she pointed down the cross street would have been comical if fear wasn't gnawing on my belly.

I was right. The fire was a distraction, but not the way I originally believed.

But I had no doubt that this time, Gerd would kill Luc.

Chapter 19

I stared at Nicholas who looked like he was about to vomit.

"He was right there, m'lady." His face turned an awful greenish yellow. "I swear!"

"Luc!" I shouted mentally and physically. That drew everyone's attention around the husk of the warehouse.

"Wardens!" Cedar Grove yelled. "Spread out! Find the high brother!" She turned back to me as Temple guards scurried to obey her.

Yanaba! I silently screamed. But it wasn't my junior justice who answered.

She fainted from the strain, Anthea, Elizabeth snapped. *I've sent for a healer. You'd better hope her child is all right.*

I blanched at the reprimand. She was totally correct. I was already exhausted myself. If I tried to do rewind now, I'd be in worse shape than Yanaba.

"Sweet Balance, what do we do now?"

The clergy and wardens' search of the surrounding warehouses proved fruitless even with the dockworkers assisting them. There was simply no trace of Luc anywhere. Even his crutches still rested in their special holster on his saddle.

Dragonfly rode down to the district accompanied by Duke Marco,

High Mother Leocadia and her staff with food and drink for those who fought the warehouse fire and searched for Luc. Both women took charge of me while Cedar Grove acceded her leadership to High Brother Han of Conflict. He admitted Thief's second had done a thorough job in trying to find Luc.

While they huddled around me across the street, Peacekeeper Jaime and his people searched the cooled down remnants of the DiRoma warehouse. Occasionally, steam hissed from inside the building when the searchers overturned debris to discover hot embers.

Temple bells clanged Second Evening in the distance. It was another half-candlemark before Jaime and the other peacekeepers exited the warehouse. He trudged toward me with something in his hands.

"This was all we found." In his left hand were cracked and broken jewels, bits of clay and bone, and a couple of dirty silver bells. In his right was a gray mass of fibers.

"Claudia!" Dragonfly cried out. Han pulled her tight against him to keep her from falling to the cobblestones.

"Wh-what about bodies?" I choked out.

Jaime shook his head, sending a cloud of ash into the air. "The sister's braids and the jewels she wore in them were all that we found. It looks like they were cut off her head. From the pattern of the burn, the fire definitely started where her hair was. The bricks beneath were cracked from the heat. The only reason there were some of the sister's braids left is her hair was so thick. But we didn't find any bodies, burned or otherwise."

"But if the fire was as hot as you say," Han prompted.

Again, Jaime shook his head, but it was Dragonfly who said, "The bits of bone you found were some of the beads that decorated Claudia's hair. There would still be some of her own bones in there if she—"

My head pounded. Why would Gerd take Luc again? The only connection between Claudia and Luc was . . .

Balance help me! My gut turned to ice as I realized Gerd's endgame. What she was going to try to force me to do.

"Chief Warden Nicholas!" I barked.

"Yes, m'lady."

"Get back to Light," I ordered. "Put the Temple on lockdown. If any of the junior clergy argue with you, summon me."

"Yes, m'lady." Nicholas sketched a quick bow before he and Tadhg took off to retrieve their horses."

"Gina, go back to Balance—" I started.

"You're going with her," Han rumbled. I opened my mouth to respond, but he waggled his index finger and said, "No arguments, Chief Justice. You're practically dead on your feet. Sister Cedar Grove, would you please go with the chief justice and her warden, and stay as an extra guard? I'll tell your high brother, and take responsibility."

"Yes, sir."

"There's no way I can convince you otherwise?" I said angrily.

Han stepped closer to me and whispered, "I fear for the babes and their mothers, too, but most especially you and Luc. Gerd's gone far beyond a simple grudge. Get some sleep. I'll call the convocation, but we'll meet at Balance in the morning. We'll start fresh then."

I couldn't argue with him. Guilt dragged me into her dark embrace, and I feared I would never see Luc again.

When we returned to the Temple District, Talbert waited for us at Balance. Cedar Grove relayed the incidents with the fire and Han's order to her.

Talbert held up his hand to calm her. "It's all right, Sister. I was actually going to suggest the same thing." He turned to me. "Brother Jeremy is not happy High Brother Luc has been abducted. Again. Young Garbhan managed to convince him Sister Shi Hua's safety takes precedence.

Ambassador Quan was kind enough to dispatch his concubine to keep the sister company through this ordeal."

I breathed a silent prayer of thanks to Balance. Talbert was one of the few people in the world who knew Yin Li's true identity. No doubt he sent word to Quan of the threat to Shi Hua's life.

Which meant he'd deduced Gerd's true agenda as well.

"We may have lost a priest, but we did gain a warden," Talbert continued. "The residents of a manor on the Temple side of Orrin found Jocasta sprawled on their courtyard flagstones and bleeding profusely from several wounds when they returned from a day at the market. Their two servants claimed they heard and saw nothing."

"Did anyone truthspell them?" I asked.

"Not yet." He shook his head. "The magistrate specifically requested you and the high brother of Light. I was about to depart for the manor house myself since the two of you were unavailable."

Gina stepped in front of me. "You really should rest, Chief Justice."

"Normally, I'd agree with you, Warden." Talbert's mouth twisted into a rueful smile. "However, the magistrate is already threatening to throw the family and their servants into the city gaol for assault. Warden Jocasta wasn't conscious. Therefore, she could not confirm or deny the events at the manor."

In the end, Talbert, Cedar Grove, and our wardens escorted me to examine the manor where the Love warden was found. I would have given anything for the strength to do a rewind when we arrived. Anything for a clue of where Gerd had taken Claudia and Luc.

"What do you mean you can't do a rewind?" DiCook shouted when I dismounted.

"Because all three of our justices have over extended themselves over the last two days, Magistrate," Cedar Grove snapped. "If we have any hope of finding our lost people, we need all of us working at full strength." The irritability of the priestess wasn't like her.

In that instant, I realized the elevation in her body temperature wasn't due to the stress and excitement of the day. My heart sank, and I prayed to Balance that Cedar Gove wasn't aware or she hadn't told anyone yet. She would be added to Gerd's list of targets the instant the knowledge got out.

High Brother Jax stalked outside of the manor house at all the shouting. "That's enough, Magistrate." He turned to me. "The family and servants' scent doesn't indicate any deception, and the only additional scent is that of Warden Jocasta. Too many peacekeepers stomped through the neighborhood for us to separate them from Jocasta's attackers."

Jax relayed the family's story to me. Thankfully, the civilians' first thought was to take poor Jocasta to the Healers Guild themselves. Unfortunately, one of the peacekeeper search parties stumbled upon them as their wagon passed through their gate.

With Talbert performing the truthspell, my interrogation of the husband, wife, their three daughters, and two servants proved unfruitful. It merely confirmed what Jax's nose and the peacekeepers report had already said.

Instead, I relied on basic physical detection. On that front, Talbert, Cedar Grove, and Jax proved to be a Twelve-send. Cedar Grove found the scratches on the gate that indicated the lock had been picked. Talbert pointed out the lack of blood on the street meant the warden had been attacked somewhere else and brought here.

We explored the manor. Even Jax claimed he couldn't hear much from the rear of the home. I sat wearily on a bench in the family's kitchen and tried to come up with an idea of what to do next.

Any idea.

"Come back here in the morning," Talbert said. "You'll be able to do a rewind once you get some rest."

"But—" I started.

"He's right, Anthea," Jax said gently. "I can station some of my people at Balance and Light to assist Chief Wardens Little Bear and Nicholas."

"No." I shook my head. "If we reduce personnel at a Temple, that will be the one she strikes at next."

"Besides, my warden and I will stay overnight at Balance," Cedar Grove said. She glared at me. "I'll make sure all three justices get some rest."

Jax frowned at first and his nose wrinkled, then the furrows on his forehead smoothed over. "Very well."

Damn. He confirmed what I suspected.

There was nothing more we could do here for the time being. I made DiCook apologize to the civilians for his people jumping to unfounded conclusions. Talbert, Jax, and I thanked them profusely on behalf of Love for coming to Warden Jocasta's aid. We gave everyone, including the servants, a silver each for the trouble we had caused them.

The Temple bells rang First Night by the time we returned to our district where we each headed for our home Temples, except for Cedar Grove and her warden. Upon our arrival at Balance, she politely asked Sivan for a pallet to be placed in my bedchamber for herself, which of course caused a little uproar amongst my own wardens.

"Stop it! All of you!" I glared at my staff and wardens, all of whom abruptly went silent. "It's too damn late and I'm too damned tired for this ruckus. A little extra magic won't hurt anyone."

"We don't need help. No one can get within the Balance walls," Warden Ahiga protested.

I cocked my head. "Sister Shi Hua."

Ahiga's skin blazed crimson as did the other wardens present. Sivan chuckled. Before the sister was formally reassigned to Orrin's Temple of Light, she was Ambassador Quan's bodyguard. She often visited me at night with none of my wardens the wiser until after she left.

I turned to Cedar Grove's warden. "Would you prefer a guest room? I'd hate for you to be infected by my wardens' shortsightedness."

"Wherever you decide is quite all right with me," he said politely.

"Good to know someone present has some manners," I said.

In the end, Ahiga volunteered his own bunk for the Thief warden, whether out of guilt or embarrassment didn't matter to me.

Once Cedar Grove and I were ensconced inside my bedchamber and I locked the door, she murmured, "You know, don't you?"

"Yes." Concern washed through me. "Is the father who I believe it to be?"

Cedar Grove grinned. "He needed to do his part, and I didn't want the priestesses at Love to have all the fun of initiating a virgin."

"But you didn't think this all the way through?" I said as I undressed.

"I admit I'm selfish. I wanted the experience," she said sheepishly as she stripped of her own clothing. She paused and stared at me. "Those of us that serve Thief and happen to be female aren't exactly encouraged to bear children. However, if I'd known a mad former priestess would want to slit my throat over my pregnancy, I would have thought twice." She frowned. "Does that make me a bad person?"

I sighed, pulled on my nightshift, and sat on my bed. "I'm in no position to judge you, Sister. That's between you, Garbhan, and the Twelve."

She merely nodded as she donned my extra nightclothes. At the shift of orange washing across her body though, I realized something else.

"You haven't told him yet, have you?" I murmured.

"I was going to wait until next month." Cedar Grove flopped onto her pallet. "But if you can see it, the Wildlings can smell it, and everyone at Thief has deduced it, though they are all too polite to say anything, then I'd better tell Garbhan sooner rather than later." She stared at the ceiling. "I wonder if our child will have pale blue eyes as well as Light talent."

"As long as your babe doesn't have blood red eyes, I'd count my blessings," I said.

We both laughed and settled in our respective beds, but we talked about the future for a long while before we both fell asleep.

Chapter 20

The next morning, I asked Elizabeth to handle court for the day. When Yanaba protested she was fine, I said, "Excellent. I will need your assistance with an outdoor rewind later."

To everyone at Balance's surprise, Leocadia and one of the new Mother wardens arrived shortly after we broke out fasts.

"I'm here to relieve Sister Cedar Grove," Leocadia said primly.

When the Thief priestess opened her mouth to argue, I smiled at her and said, "Please relay my gratitude to your high brother for assisting me, and if you care to visit with me again, I would definitely look forward to it. However, you mentioned a task you needed to accomplish today, and I don't want to delay you."

Cedar Grove's face flushed bright orange, and she bowed. "Thank you, Chief Justice."

When she turned to leave, her warden paused next to me and whispered, "You also have the gratitude of Thief. That's the calmest she's been in the last four weeks." He winked at me before he followed his priestess out of my Temple.

Leocadia frowned after him before she looked at me. "Am I missing something here?"

"Quite a bit." I grinned at her. "But it's not my truth to share."

A wry smile crossed the high mother's face. "I hate to be the one to inform you, but you cannot fulfill the edict without a man."

For once, the absurdity of my situation made me chuckle instead of making me want to break something. "I hate to be the one to inform you, but I cannot fulfill the edict even with a man."

Leocadia stammered. "My apologies for my attempt at humor hurting you."

"No, High Mother, I could use your attempt at levity after the past two days." I smiled at her. "I was about to leave for some investigative work. Would you like to accompany me?"

"I would be honored." She looked relieved I wasn't going to hold her misstep against her. But then, she had offered the proverbial sheaf of maize. I wasn't about ruin the gesture of peace when I needed all the allies I could get.

I took Warden Daniel with me to the manor where Jocasta had been found. He'd become quite adept at witnessing a rewind for me.

"You use your wardens as witnesses?" High Mother Leocadia asked as we rode east across the city.

"Renegades keep killing our Light priests," I replied. "And I've been running the handful I have left ragged over the last few months. Not to mention I keep losing one in particular." Luc's disappearance wasn't funny, but if I didn't let my dark sense of humor flow, I would end up in my bed, weeping like I had as a child when I was first taken to Standora. Such an action would help no one.

Leocadia shook her head. "How did things go so wrong in Orrin?"

"My predecessor went senile, and my Reverend Mother refused to replace her." I inhaled deeply and released the air. "Some folks here did their best to keep the chaos at bay. Others took advantage of the chaos to further their own ends."

"You mean Bianca," Leocadia said bitterly.

"Or Gerd." I glanced at the priestess. "High Father Jerrod did tell you she is my birth mother, didn't he?"

"He . . . mentioned it," Leocadia grudgingly admitted.

I chuckled. "He's still furious I kept him under house arrest."

"Is that what you would do with me?" she asked.

"Only if you committed a crime, or I was trying to protect you because I'm the one balancing on the legal line."

"And which one was Jerrod?"

I looked at Leocadia. "He still has his head, doesn't he?"

Her burst of laughter caught us both by surprise. "I apologize for being a fool, Chief Justice."

"Just don't deal in demon artifacts or sell children, and you'll be fine."

Unfortunately, my rewind at the manor house where Warden Jocasta was found yielded few new clues. The people who picked the gate lock and dumped Jocasta on the flagstones wore masks and hoods. As my own Warden Daniel said, the pair were between my height and his, so they were likely men. Once again, I apologized to the residents, and they expressed their gratitude they had been cleared of assaulting a Temple warden.

Since we weren't too far from the Healers Guild, we rode in that direction next.

"Do you often check on the wardens of other Temples?" Leocadia asked as we steered our mounts around clusters of foot traffic.

"Jocasta is a witness to a crime," I said. "Every possible lead needs to be followed."

Again, the priestess shook her head. "I never realized how much a justice did."

"It's not all pronouncing judgments and cutting off heads." I gestured around us. “Unfortunately, that’s the part of our duties most are aware of.”

“Or is it you’re more capable than most justices?”

A suspicious sound came from behind me I knew damn well wasn’t made by my warden’s horse.

I glanced over my shoulder, but Daniel stared straight ahead with a neutral expression on his face. I looked at Leocadia again.

“That snort from Warden Daniel indicates I’m more stubborn than most justices.” I sighed. “I wish I could only blame him, but the other eleven wardens at Balance would have made the same noise if they were with us.”

“My Reverend Mother would have had our wardens lashed for such a mockery,” Leocadia said softly.

“So would mine, but I have asked my wardens to speak their minds.” I looked and grinned at Daniel before I turned back to Leocadia. “I’ve found it keeps me alive.”

When we arrived at the Healers Guild, the guild chief Master Healer Aaron escorted us back to Jocasta’s room. The poor warden looked awful from the combination of the heated skin and increased blood circulation on the left side of her head and her left arm. He asked for the warden’s permission to tell me the list of her injuries and treatments, which she gave willingly.

But before he could speak, she blurted, “Have you found Sister Claudia yet?”

“That’s what I hoped to talk to you about.” I looked at Aaron. “If she’s well enough for a conversation, that is.”

“If the situation wasn’t so dire, I’d say no.” He grimaced. “No truth spells, Anthea. We worked too hard to keep her alive.”

“I don’t doubt you,” I said. “Tell me everything.”

Aaron ticked off the injuries. "Double fracture of the left forearm. A cracked skull and lower jaw. A bladed puncture to her left lung."

Anger boiled through my veins. "In other words, they thought they'd killed her."

Aaron nodded. "Luckily, we now have plenty of experience healing your head wounds. As I told High Sister Dragonfly, another day of observation and a few days of rest at the Temple, she'll be good as new." He patted the warden's foot and started to leave before he shot me a mock glare. "I mean it, Anthea, no truth spells on the poor girl."

Jocasta grimaced at being called a child. I didn't blame her.

"I promise. No truth spells. I need my energy for another rewind." I made shooing motions with my hands, and Aaron left chuckling as he closed the door.

I took a seat in the chair beside the warden. "How are you truly feeling, Jocasta?"

She blinked in surprise at my familiarity. "I'm fine. Do the truthspell. Please. You need to find Sister Claudia."

"First of all, she's not the only clergyperson who's been abducted." I took her left hand in both of mine. "Second of all, I trust Gina, and she trusts you. That's good enough for me."

Jocasta nodded and swallowed hard. "Where would you like me to begin?"

"Your high sister said Sister Claudia had a pain in her abdomen, and you were escorting Claudia to the Healers Guild," I prompted.

"I drove the wagon down Oak Street since it has far less traffic in the late afternoon." She reached for the cup on the table to her right and took a long drink. I pictured the layout of the streets in my mind. Oak Street was two blocks west of where Jocasta had been found, so the renegades hadn't gone far to dispose of her.

"We had just passed Plum Court when I heard a muffled cry from the sister and felt a jolt to the wagon. I started to turn around when I saw something coming toward my head. I automatically raised my arm."

Jocasta started trembling, and I coaxed a little calming magic into her. She took a deep breath before she continued.

"I heard my bones crack. I reached for my dagger, but the war hammer struck my head before I could pull it free."

"Did you see the faces of the people who attacked you?" I asked.

She started to shake her head and quickly found it was an ill-advised gesture after a head injury, even a healed one. "There were two of them. They wore masks over their noses and mouths, and their hoods were pulled low. They were dressed as Death Wardens."

It wasn't the first time the renegades had used Temple disguises. Bianca had furnished them clothing for the Twelve knew how long.

"Do you remember anything after they hit you in the head?"

"I woke in the wagon. Sister Claudia lay beside me, gagged and bound in shackles. A mourning sheet had been thrown over us. I whispered to her to stay alive for her child's sake no matter what." A tear rolled down Jocasta's cheek, and she cleared her throat.

"Unfortunately, I think one of the renegades heard me. It was a man's voice that said, 'The warden is still alive. What do we do?' Another man answered, 'Kill her and dump the body like she said.' That's when one of them stabbed me in the back. I couldn't breathe properly, and I passed out. The next thing I remember was waking up here this morning."

I considered Jocasta's words. A "she" was giving orders. Possibly Gerd. Or maybe it was whoever Gerd reported to. Jocasta's death was supposed to be another distraction for me. So why abduct Luc? Unless the renegades merely wanted me to be chasing my tail while they assassinated the remaining Light clergy and anyone carrying a possible Light child.

"Can you think of anything else your attackers said?" I asked.

Jocasta stared at the ceiling of her room. "I wish I could. Demon take them, I wish I knew how they got behind me."

"If you were on Oak Street, my guess is they were perched in the trees," I said. "We humans forget to look up."

"But how would they know I'd bring the sister that way?" Jocasta raised her hands helplessly. "For that matter, how would they know about her pains?"

"Those are two very good questions, my dear Warden." I squeezed her hand and pushed to my feet. "And I intend to find answers to both of them."

Chapter 21

When Leocadia, our wardens, and I exited through the Healers Guild's main gate on horseback, Magistrate DiCook and two of his peacekeepers waited outside in a wagon. I didn't recognize the one driving, but Peacekeeper Leyti rode in the back. DiCook climbed down and rocked back on his heels as he eyed the high mother. It was his indication he was troubled.

"Have you so worn out the clergy of Balance and Light you need to recruit assistance from the other Temples, Chief Justice?" He was trying to tease, but he brought my denied emotions crashing down on me.

"I have two missing clergy members, the murders of a Temple head of household and a warden, and the attempted murder of another warden, Magistrate. Please do not try my patience today." I willed myself to calm down a hair. "Why are you here?"

"I went to Balance, but Chief Warden Little Bear wouldn't even let me inside."

"I have both Balance and Light locked down for now."

DiCook's eyes narrowed. "You figured out her real goal."

"I believe so, but the task is finding her before she completes it."

He nodded. "Your chief warden said you were going to the house were Warden Jocasta was found. I figured you'd come here next to talk to her. How's she doing?"

"About as well as to be expected, considering the renegades tried to bash in her skull and stabbed her for good measure," I said.

DiCook stroked his beard. "What's next?"

"Why?" I bit out.

He stepped closer and lowered his voice. "Anthea, I'm on your side, and I want to help. However, if you don't wish my assistance, have the courtesy to say it to my face instead of playing word games."

Once again, I was taking my fear and frustration out on someone who had proven himself. And DiCook had as much reason to want Gerd's head on a platter as I did. "I'm heading down to the DiRoma warehouse."

"Mind if I accompany you and your party, Chief Justice?" he asked incredibly politely. Which was unusual for our odd, fractious, yet close, relationship.

"That would be acceptable," I replied.

While DiCook climbed back onto the wagon, Leocadia leaned close to me and whispered, "Why is he insisting on coming with us?"

"Truly?" I asked.

She nodded.

"He doesn't trust you, and he doesn't want to have to train a new justice if you kill me." I grinned at her shocked expression at my blatant blasphemy.

Finally, she shook her head as we followed the peacekeeper's wagon. "No wonder Orrin is in so much trouble."

"Actually, we're in trouble because no one questioned the problems with our predecessors," I muttered. "Mine was senile. Yours was a criminal, as was Love's. Light's was too fond of drink. The only righteous one of the bunch was High Sister Bertrice, and she sacrificed her life to save the citizens of Tandor from a demon army."

At my blunt assessment, Leocadia remained quiet all the way across the city.

When we arrived at the burned out hulk of the former DiRoma warehouse on Fishlock Street, the acrid scent of ashes and smoke still tainted the air. High Brother Han of Conflict had left the sister who'd questioned Luc and two Conflict wardens to watch the area.

DiCook jumped down from the wagon. "Where do you want spotters, Chief Justice?"

"Would you be willing to go inside the warehouse, Magistrate?" I asked as I dismounted Nassa. He'd acted as a witness for me before, so he knew the routine.

"I assumed you'd have Justice Yanaba rewind the entire block." He frowned as he stroked his beard.

"I am, but someone left Sister Claudia's braids in there." I pointed at the remains of the warehouse.

The Conflict priestess and her two wardens approached us and bowed. "Sister Migina, Chief Justice," the priestess said. "We are here to serve. The high brother said to follow your instructions implicitly."

"Your service is greatly appreciated." I inclined my head before I addressed the group. "Two of you have witnessed for me before. For the rest of you, this is a new experience. All you will be seeing are images of the past. None of these things can hurt you. If a trap spell has been set, I'll be the one at whom it will be aimed."

DiCook frowned at my last statement, no doubt reminded of the trap spell that had been set on the orphan Yellow Fin's corpse. The force of it had knocked over the magistrate and all of the wardens and peacekeepers observing the rewind. At least, DiCook remained silent about that little fact.

"The magistrate will stand inside the walls of the warehouse with the Conflict personnel and Peacekeeper Leyti at each of the corners. Especially watch for anyone going inside or coming out of the warehouse," I instructed. The five of them nodded. Leyti seemed surprised I remembered his name.

"Warden Daniel, stand over there on that side street." I pointed to where our horses had been last night. "That's the last place anyone saw High Brother Luc. Peacekeeper?" I gestured at the one whose name I didn't know.

"Fat Squirrel, Lady Justice," he said.

I looked his scrawny form up and down.

"It's the name I was given as a baby since I had quite the appetite." He smiled and shrugged. "I've kept it as my public name."

"All right," I said noncommittally. It simply wasn't my business to tell someone what name they could use in public. I placed him on the same side street as Daniel, but on the opposite side of Fishlock Street.

"High Mother, would you and your warden please stand at the other intersection?" I pointed at the next side street to the north.

Leocadia nodded and asked, "What are we looking for?"

I frowned and looked around us. "Anything that seems out of place. Someone too interested in the fire, or not interested enough. An animal not running from the blaze. But most especially High Brother Luc or Sister Claudia."

"Very well, Chief Justice," Leocadia said. Our group of witnesses moved to their positions.

Yanaba?

I'm ready, my junior justice said. *Elizabeth is here with me.*

Be careful, I said silently. *I don't want your brains fried by a trap spell.*

That's why I'm here, Elizabeth grumbled.

The prickle of a rewind spell traveled across my skin. The strands of time jumped back less than a day. No blackness rushed out of the past.

Of course not. Gerd probably didn't know about Yanaba's connection with the city. Or maybe Gerd was concerned I'd detect her use of demon magic here.

Pale blue wisps moved past me. Even with my odd sight, I could barely detect the people and animals moving around the street. I still had to depend on normal-sighted folks to know what was happening in the past.

"A wagon with two men has pulled up in front of the warehouse," Peacekeeper Leyti called out. "One of them jumps down from the wagon. He picks the padlock and opens the doors."

Damn. It wouldn't take much to open a simple industrial padlock, especially if those two men were trained in the same techniques as the clergy of Thief.

"They are dressed as common dockworkers," Sister Migina added as she stepped closer to the image she observed. "The driver guides the horses inside, and the other one closes the warehouse doors."

DiCook picked up the narrative. With the doors in ashes and the roof collapsed, I could hear him clearly. "They are unloading a wrapped item from the bed of the wagon. It's Sister Claudia. She's bound with manacles and gagged."

Spell-threaded bonds to prevent her from fighting back? I wasn't going to ask where they obtained them. Any of the traitor clergy could have provided them.

"What the demon!" DiCook spluttered a few more obscenities.

"Witness for me, Magistrate!" I yelled at him.

"There's a hatch in the floor." He grabbed a few partially burned timbers and piled them to mark the spot. "The two men took the sister down through the hatch. I can't see them!"

I could understand the magistrate's frustration.

Speed up the forward time, I said silently to Yanaba.

"The two men are coming back up," DiCook called out.

Slow down the rewind, I relayed to Yanaba.

"One of them has something in his hand," DiCook said. "Braids with beads on the ends, just like Sister Claudia's. He retrieves a jar from the wagon and drops the hair on the middle of the floor. It looks like he's pouring oil over the braids. He tosses the jar aside and it smashes against the bricks. Now's he dumping sand, no, grain on the oil and braids. The two of them scatter kindling and straw around the floors. They're opening the doors and backing the wagon and horse out of the warehouse."

"They're heading north on Fishlock Street," Sister Migina said.

Sweet Balance, was Claudia still buried beneath the burned rubble of the warehouse? My gut churned. Last night, we had no reason to believe anyone was inside when the fire started.

Speed up the forward time again, I said to Yanaba. I could feel the strain on her and Elizabeth feeding her energy. All three of us were near the limits of our collective endurance. If Yanaba lost her hold on the spell, we'd need to wait another day to perform the rewind.

I didn't think Gerd would keep Luc or Claudia alive that much longer.

DiCook jumped and swore very loudly. "The braids have ignited. Mother!" He ducked and covered his head from the invisible flames. "There was enough grain dust in here it blew up like Jing flash powder."

I stepped away from the entrance to the warehouse and headed closer to where Daniel stood.

"Your party has arrived," my warden said.

The others called out the actions on the street including the insane effort by me and Sister Cedar Grove to put out the blaze. But it was Daniel I wanted a clue, a suggestion, anything to tell me how Luc disappeared last night.

At the point in the timeline where the mist and smoke envelope the street, Daniel shouts, "A hooded and masked figure stepped out of this warehouse!" The warden had a hard time keeping his emotions under control during a rewind, but I wasn't about to berate him. Not now. Not when my entire body vibrated with my own fear and anxiety.

"He yanked High Brother Luc off his horse and slapped a cloth over his mouth and nose," Daniel continued. "The high brother has become unconscious. The figure drags the high brother into the warehouse."

Daniel knocked on the wooden wall until the pitch changed. "Here." His fingers probed around the edges.

The door must be cleverly hidden from those with normal sight. Without the fire affecting the surrounding buildings, I could detect the fine temperature difference of air traveling through the cracks around the hidden door.

Yanaba, speed up the rewind.

She did so, but none of my witnesses observed anything we didn't already know. Time snapped back into place. However, mine and Daniel's attention was still on the hidden door.

"I think this is the trigger." Daniel reach for what appeared to be a knothole, but there was a blue flash of steel inside.

"No!" I grabbed his wrist and yanked him back.

"What—"

"There's a needle, and knowing the Assassins Guild it's probably poisoned." I crouched before the hidden door to examine the mechanism.

"What did you find?" DiCook asked at the same time Yanaba said, *I'm taking a nap now.*

Thank you, Yanaba. We found what we were looking for, I said before I looked up at DiCook. "They drugged Luc and pulled him through this hidden door the instant the roof collapsed. Now we know why Gerd stole the vial of soma from Vintner. Unfortunately, they've laid a trap for us."

"If the renegades expect us to go in one way, we need to go another," Peacekeeper Leyti said. "The rewind showed enough legal reason for us to gain access to this warehouse, right?"

I nodded.

"Then follow me." Leyti headed back towards the street. We all trailed after him. He retrieved two hatchets from the peacekeeper wagon and tossed one to his colleague before he marched into the wide-open doors of the warehouse.

The workers inside stared at our entire group. A man who must have been the foreman with his puffed up chest and equally puffed up attitude charged up to us.

"Here now! What do you lot think you're doing—" He stopped abruptly when I pushed back my hood. "Ch-chief Justice." He gulped loudly. "How may I serve?"

"You and your workers line up over there." I pointed at the piles of boxes lining the opposing wall. "Sister Migina, would you and your wardens please watch them?"

"With pleasure," the priestess bit out. She and her wardens drew their swords. "Move it!" she roared, and the dockworkers and their foreman scrambled to obey.

Leyti counted off paces along the southern wall and stopped in front of another pile of boxes. He looked at Daniel. "About here, right, Warden?"

At Daniel's nod, the rest of us shifted the shipping containers away from the spot. Even Leocadia pitched in and helped. My opinion of her was improving by the second. Bianca would never have deigned to dirty her robes in any manner, much less volunteer to do physical labor.

Once enough space was clear, Leyti and the other peacekeeper started hacking at the wall.

"Hey, you can't—" With Migina's swordpoint at his throat, the foreman whined, "Sister, they can't destroy this building. The owner will be—"

"Compensated for the damage or under arrest," I snapped. "Now, do be quiet before I arrest you for obstructing justice."

The foreman closed his mouth. Obviously, he decided he'd rather face his employer's wrath than the lash.

"I think we found how the renegades stole away with the high brother," DiCook said.

I ducked my head through the hole the peacekeepers had made. The hidden door was more obvious as was the space between the outside and inside walls. It was big enough for a full-grown man to stand inside with his shoulders barely touching each wall.

And on the floor among the dust and wood chips was another trap door.

Chapter 22

I swung one leg through the hole into the hidden space when DiCook grabbed my arm. I looked at his hand and then at his face.

"I don't give a rat's ass about propriety, Anthea," he hissed. "You're not going first. You're at the top of the Assassins Guild's list."

"But I know what I'm looking for magically," I said. "You don't and can't."

He released my arm, acquiescing to my point. I stretched out my senses, but I didn't detect the alien feel of demon magic. However, I did recognize the scent of flash powder. And the bitter almond of the Assassins Guild's favorite poison.

I closed my eyes and concentrated. *Sister Cedar Grove?*

Yes, Chief Justice? She tried to conceal her surprise, but even a surface mental link like silent speech conveyed emotions.

Please tell your high brother I need assistance disarming an Assassins Guild lock trap. We discovered how High Brother Luc was abducted last night. It's a tight space and I don't want anyone poisoning themselves by accident.

Right away, Lady Justice, she answered.

"Magistrate, would you please have one of your people watch the side street?" I grimaced. "We don't need anyone accidentally poisoning themselves before someone from Thief can disarm that external trigger."

I pulled my other leg through the opening and crouched next to the trap door on the floor. My fingertips carefully traced the edges. Cooler air puffed up from below, but it wasn't the icy feel of a cold room. I stretched out on my belly in the dust, drew my dagger and lifted the door with the tips of my fingers.

The colder air from below ground made the trigger strings stand out blue against the yellow-green wood. Carefully, I sliced the strings on each side of the door, then lifted it until it slammed down on the other side of the opening, raising a cloud of dust.

I turned my head away, but that didn't stop a healthy round of sneezing.

Finally, I stopped long enough to peer into the hole. Two flashbangs hung from the wooden framework of the door. The string attached to the flashbangs were to keep them in place, not to be used as wicks. There were no friction sources to light the strings either.

Unless the friction source for a spark was inside the flashbangs.

"Magistrate?" I looked up at DiCook's head poking through the hole in the south wall. "Would you find a sturdy container and packing material? There's a couple of unusual flashbangs here I'm sure Thief and Conflict will want to study."

DiCook's face yellowed and his bellowed orders echoed through the hidden passageway.

By the time I delicately cut the odd flashbangs from the frame, extra wardens and priests arrived from Balance, Thief, and Conflict.

"You were supposed to keep her out of trouble," Little Bear growled at Daniel.

"If you can't, how do you expect your junior wardens to succeed?" I smiled to take the sting out of my words. It was obvious the poor man was frustrated beyond belief.

Talbert made fairly quick work of the locking mechanism. Once he was out of the way, I climbed into the space and scrambled down the ladder before anyone could stop me.

Leocadia followed me down before her own warden or the male priests could object.

"How can you see down here?" she grumbled.

"I don't see like the rest of you," I commented.

"I know that." But she dropped the subject when she closed her eyes. A familiar tingle ran across my skin.

"How can you create a light ball?" I asked in wonder.

"Women can't be inducted into the Temple of Light," she said sourly. "The Reverend Mothers and Fathers had to figure out where else to place me."

I shook my head. "You are just full of surprises, High Mother."

Little Bear and Leocadia's warden joined us in what we quickly learned was a tunnel. On the east side, it only traveled as far as the burnt DiRoma warehouse. This was where the renegades had taken Claudia. We found a silver bell half-buried in the dirt.

But we couldn't see an end to the western direction, so we started walking that way. Leocadia and I kept in contact with the clergy waiting topside through silent speech. As we continued, the tunnel gradually slopped downward, and the walls became damp.

"This place probably floods during high tide," Little Bear commented.

"Next high tide will be around Second Afternoon," the Mother warden murmured.

"All right." I calculated silently. "Another thousand steps and then we'll return. Personally, I don't feel like drowning today."

It was less then two hundred steps when we heard sea waves crashing against the shore. We hurried our pace. Sun warmed my face when I stepped around a rock. A beach lay before us. Sea birds cried out their displeasure at the interruption of their privacy.

"Sandy Spit?" Little Bear looked around in amazement.

"Sandy Spit?" Leocadia repeated with a confused expression.

"It's one of the best places for clamming, High Mother," her warden answered. "But I thought the only way to access it was by sea."

"But how did anyone not know about this?" Leocadia asked.

Little Bear snorted. "You grow up along the coast you learn to be careful exploring sea caves."

I turned around and looked up. A sheer cliff face extended straight up, easily ten or more stories. Then I began cursing in every language I could think of.

"They knew! The damn renegades knew we'd eventually close the demon-damned tunnels, so they dug new ones to get in and out of the city!"

The other three looked at me like I'd gone insane. Perhaps I was.

"Anthea!" Little Bear seized my shoulders and shook me. "Pull yourself together! They couldn't have gone far. Not carrying two people."

I looked at him, and the regret and desire flashed across his face. And it was all my fault because I couldn't control myself around other Temples' magic and kissed him. He released me, but said no more.

The sand suddenly gained my interest. "They could have had a ship offshore with a long boat waiting here on the beach during the last low tide," I said more quietly.

"Gerd's not going to take them that far," Leocadia stepped closer to us. "Not if she plans to use them against Orrin."

"True," Little Bear said. "Killing anyone with Light talent and using their deaths to fuel a spell would be something she would do. They could have simply held the high brother inside the space between the walls if he were drugged as the rewind showed. They waited until the fire was out and everyone left."

"But if they tried to take him out through the secret door, we would have seen them during the rewind," I protested.

Anthea? Leocadia? Elizabeth sounded tired. *Talbert found a second secret door in the warehouse.*

We wasted the rest of the afternoon questioning the warehouse workers and their supervisor. It turned out the second warehouse was owned by Lord Aleister DeGrove of Pana Valley. However, it had been rented by the Temples of Love, Mother, and Vintner over the last year. The workers currently there knew nothing, though the foreman seemed rather overjoyed he wasn't going mad. Apparently, his exterior and interior calculated volumes never added up correctly, and Lord Aleister had accused him of theft.

As Han said, Gerd or Bianca could have altered the building while they were leasing it.

Talbert's second door was on the back side of the warehouse. He pointed out from the disturbed dust, the renegades could have taken Luc and Claudia out that way.

So in the end, I returned to Balance no further ahead in this blasted investigation than when I started. Now, two clergy were missing and a warden was dead. I had just finished cleaning up and changed into a clean uniform when someone knocked on my bedchamber door.

"Come in!"

However, it wasn't Sivan with my midday meal. Nathan entered with a very serious look on his face.

"What can I do for you, my squire?" I forced a smile because I surely wasn't going to take my horrible mood out on any child, much less Nathan.

"I just return from Master Govind's with a message," he said gravely. "Cat says she found where Gerd's hiding."

Chapter 23

My entire body quivered at Nathan's news. "Where?"

"She was afraid to tell Govind. She said for you to meet her at the Ash Pile at First Evening by yourself, and she'd show you."

I frowned. The Ash Pile was the city's communal disposal for wood ashes from fireplaces and cook stoves. Farmers from the duchy came for the ashes to use as fertilizer. Normally, I would say it would be impossible for Gerd and her accomplices to hide there. But then, I walked to Sandy Spit earlier today, and I would have said that was impossible when I awoke this morning.

"All right." I nodded. "The Ash Pile at First Evening."

"I know she said to go by yourself—" Nathan started.

"Don't worry, good sir." I clasped his shoulder. "I've learned to listen to your wise counsel. I promise I won't go by myself."

Cedar Grove relayed Talbert's findings and plan shortly after Third Afternoon. *I delivered your package to the high brother. We are set on this end. Brother Sisquoc will be with you the entire way. Whatever Gerd tries, we'll be watching your back.*

I repeated Cedar Grove's report to Little Bear and Gina who sat across my desk. Both of them crossed their arms over their chests and glared at me.

"I still don't like this," Little Bear muttered. "We don't know what other secret exits she has planted through the city."

"Of course, it's a trap." Gina's disgruntlement spread thickly across her words. "The only thing we can do is spring it and see what happens."

"You should be taking all of us with you," Little Bear grumbled.

"I'll be up against demon magic, my friend," I said. "I will not have Sivan hounding me through eternity for getting you or anyone else from Balance killed."

"What bothers us is you trust the Tandoran Wildling more than you trust us," Gina spat.

"No, Sisquoc knows what he's getting into, and he has more experience in fighting demons and skinwalkers," I said with all the calm I could muster.

"Then you'd better not get yourself killed either," Little Bear growled. "Because I'll help Sivan resurrect you from the dead just to yell at you myself."

At half a candlemark before First Evening, I set out on foot towards the Ash Pile. As I rounded the corner at the Temple of Love, a panther stepped away from the wall and prowled by my side. Sisquoc's fur probably blended in for normally sighted people, but to me, he was a deep green color.

"Thank you for coming," I whispered. He butted his head against my thigh.

I hadn't talked with the Wildling priest much since he'd been transferred to Orrin. He probably missed High Brother Aduba of Conflict terribly.

We turned onto Oak Street and had just passed Peach Court when I saw two renegades perched on branches in the trees ahead. I stopped well away from them and stared. Someone had definitely tipped them off regarding our route. Part of me hoped it wasn't Leocadia.

"Really?" I said. "You're going to try the same trick twice?"

Sisquoc coughed a warning and sprang to the left. I dove to the right, rolled, and came up with my sword in my hand. Three renegades had managed to come in behind us. And I had been worried this trip would be boring.

Migina! I yelled silently.

Mounted Conflict clergy and wardens thundered down Oak Street from the north, but they were a few moments late. I ducked the swing of a war hammer. The two other renegades tried to corner Sisquoc. I ducked another swing and slashed at my opponent's midriff.

The two idiots in the tree clambered down. One of them had something in his hand, but I was too busy keeping my skull intact until it was too late. He threw some powdered substance in my face. A wave of dizziness hit me, and I went down on one knee.

Powdered soma.

Then the Conflict horses surrounded me, but something was wrong. It felt like I was seeing the world through a Love sister's veil. My fingers didn't work, and I could no longer hold my sword. Someone dragged me across the cobblestones.

The Conflict wardens yelled at each other when they discovered I wasn't there. Sister Migina picked up my sword and looked wildly around her, but she couldn't see me. I tried to call out to her. A fist struck my cheek, and I stared up at a face similar to my own, but with a much smaller nose.

Damn, I thought as consciousness slipped from my grasp. The bitch truly does have the ability to cloak herself.

Chapter 24

The Twelve awful smell of rotten meat dragged me back into consciousness. My shoulders ached, and my head throbbed.

"Anthea? Anthea, you need to wake up," someone whispered nearby. Someone I should know.

I forced my eyes open. That action did not help my stomach one bit. Someone was hanging from chains next to me. "Luc?"

My head lolled to the other side. Across the room, someone else hung from chains on a rail. Claudia. All of her beautiful hair was gone. From the cuts on her scalp and the bruises on her face, her abductors had been none too gentle when they sliced off her braids.

The scent, the chains, and the rails finally clicked in my aching head. We were in a butcher's shop. I think I should have been scared, but I was very happy.

"Thank the Twelve, you two are alive," I murmured.

"We won't be for long," Luc hissed. "Does anyone know where you are? These damn shackles are spell-threaded."

Spell-threaded with demon magic I realized when I tried to speak to Luc silently.

I started to answer Luc aloud, but I stopped. A third person stood in the doorway. I blinked away the moisture running down my face. "Cat?"

"Lovely little street mice you have, my darling daughter." The last words were said with more of a sneering insult than with care from the blurry figure behind the girl.

Gerd. The color of her skin wasn't the grey-green of a true skinwalker, but it was awfully close.

I glared at my birth mother, or I tried to. "Wh-what did you do to them?"

"Possession is such an interesting experience." Her smile sent chills down my spine. Or maybe it was the demon magic in the chains biting into my flesh. She entered the room. In one hand, she held a leash attached to a collar around Dog's neck. The boy was crawling on all fours behind her. In Gerd's other hand, she held a silk-wrapped bundle.

"I can literally be in several places at once."

"You know you're just a tool to them," I said.

"Not after tonight." She smirked. "Your friends killed the idiots sent to keep an eye on me. And I needed three sacrifices to fuel the destruction of Orrin, which will give me unlimited power. Sit," she ordered. Dog sat on his haunches. "Good boy." She patted his head.

My heart threatened to explode from my chest when I saw what she was unwrapping. The demon grimoire. The same one Sister Gretchen had stolen from her. The same one I turned over to the Reverend Mother for disposal. The same one Yanaba swore had been destroyed.

"H-how—"

"How did it get back to me?" Gerd asked innocently. "It knows its true master." She stroked the cover as if it were a lover's body before she flipped open to a page somewhere in the middle of the grimoire. Mumbling words in the demon's language rolled from her tongue.

I could feel the alien energy building. Both Luc and I yanked on our chains, trying to break free. Gerd drew a knife from her belt, still chanting, as she approached Claudia.

"You demon!" Claudia spat at Gerd.

"Almost." Gerd plunged the knife into the priestess's abdomen. Claudia screamed, and the world exploded in a flash of white light.

Chapter 25

I dropped to the floor, my wrists burning as I tried to shake off the shackles. The metal flaked away like ash, and the demon magic in the chains no longer blurred my mind. I was free.

Gerd screamed and whirled away from Claudia. Her knife clattered against the concrete floor, and the grimoire landed with a thud. The only thing worse than Claudia bleeding out on the floor was Gerd's face.

Or half that had been burned away.

"Anthea!" Luc was sprawled on the floor, but my idiot birth mother hadn't disarmed him. He tossed me his sword.

With both of my hands on the grip, I pivoted and swung with all my strength. Gerd's head bounced once and rolled away. Her body fell over sideways. Luc crawled over to Claudia and tried to staunch the blood from her wound.

The prickly sensation of tiny kitten claws all over my skin said we'd been found. I picked up the grimoire. It shrank in my hands. I quickly wrapped it in its silk, tucked it in the back waistband of my leggings and covered it with my robes before I called out to Talbert to let him know Claudia needed medical help.

Talbert took charge because neither Luc or I were in any condition to do so. Cat and Dog were both in shock since Gerd had her psychic claws in them when she died. Han had his people take the children straight to Child.

The High Brother of Thief had also thought ahead. Master Healer Bly and her apprentice were there with a wagon. The Temple personnel quickly loaded Claudia and Luc in the cushioned bed before they raced toward the Healers Guild manor houses.

I snapped at anyone who came near me, except for Migina when she returned my sword. Physically, I was fine, other than a few bruises from Gerd dragging me across the cobblestones of Oak Street and an abominable headache from the soma powder the renegades drugged me with. I crouched in the corner of the butcher's killing room and watched while DiCook directed the collection of evidence.

Not that it mattered. The two assassins with Gerd who survived the initial clash with the Conflict wardens managed to commit suicide when they saw the tide had turned against them. Only after Sister Raven Claw and her wardens salted and collected Gerd's corpse did I let DiCook drive me to the Healers Guild.

When we arrived, one of the guild journeywomen escorted us to a waiting area. Luc sat in the room with Warden Yar standing by his chair.

I sat beside him while DiCook sat across the room to give us a token semblance of privacy.

"Are you all right?" I asked softly.

"Just bruises." He stared at the floor, not even looking at me.

"Did they give you anything to eat?"

"I'm not hungry."

"They dug another tunnel out of the city," I said. Why wouldn't he look at me?

"So I heard."

"What you need from me?" I murmured.

He finally looked at me. "Nothing. Not a damn thing." His voice was cold.

Colder than a demon's touch.

Dragonfly rushed into the room and to Luc's side. "Any word yet?"

He shook his head.

She sat beside DiCook, and we all waited in that uncomfortable silence.

According to the oil lamp in the waiting area, a full candlemark passed before a weary Master Healer Aaron walked in. We all rose, the tension thick.

"Claudia?" Dragonfly clutched her hands to her chest.

"She's alive," Aaron said. "Her recovery is going to take time. The demon magic did a lot of damage, but she'll live."

"The baby?" Luc asked.

Aaron shook his head and whispered, "I'm sorry."

I couldn't handle Luc's flood of grief. I rushed out of the room and into the night.

Chapter 26

DiCook caught up with me and insisted on driving me back to Balance. At least, that's what I think happened. It wouldn't be the first time I was wrong.

I entered my bedchamber and locked the door. I didn't need Sivan, Nathan, or one of the wardens interrupting me. If anyone felt what I was doing, I would say I was destroying a personal article contaminated with demon essence.

The unintelligible whispers in the back of my mind grew more urgent. I needed to hide the damn grimoire. If I took it back to Standora for destruction, it would only end up in the hands of the renegades' spy at the home Temple again.

I pulled the grimoire from where I tucked it in the back waistband of my leggings. Now that the tunnel system was shut down, it would be the safest place to store the grimoire until I could figure out how to use it against the renegades.

The grimoire grew back to its full size once I removed it from under my robes. Did the demon used to bind the grimoire retain its abilities to change shape as well? It didn't really matter. If I learned how it seduced people, I could develop a counterspell.

I examined the wall where the original passage into the tunnel was. Yanaba had shattered the spell thoroughly. There was no way I could reuse that block of marble. But I didn't want someone to find the new access by accident either.

Fortunately, my new wardrobe was smaller and lighter. I had also ordered a new trunk for my new weapons since Yanaba destroyed all of my old belongings when she activated the Temple's defensive spells last spring. My only regret about that incident is we lost our copies of a rare tome by High Brother Euclid of Kemet.

My thoughts were drifting again. I pulled the wardrobe away from the wall, stripped off my cloak and boots, and sat before the marble slab behind the wardrobe's normal resting place. Magic flowed from me and around me as I recreated the spell to fold back the marble. I wasn't sure how long I worked, but my limbs trembled, and my skin was slick with sweat by the time I finished.

When I said the words to open the passage for the first time, my heart jumped with relief. A slimy feeling covered my flesh even through the silk when I picked up the demon grimoire and set it inside the tunnel. I closed the passage, but I could still hear the horrid thing whispering to me.

However, I was too tired to care. I stripped off my leggings and tunic and dropped on my bed. Normally, when I was this troubled, I could share my cares with Luc. But I couldn't this time. Not when he and Claudia were consumed by grief for their lost child. I curled up under my light blanket and pretended the moisture running down my cheeks was perspiration.

If you are enjoying the adventures of Anthea and the people of the Justice universe, drop me a line through my website (www.suzanharden.com) Twitter (@ Suzan_Harden), or Facebook (SuzanHardenWriter). Recommending the Justice series to your friends or writing a review would be even better.

Turn the page for a sneak preview of the next Justice story!

A Virtue of Child

I jerked out of a sound sleep, a scream at the back of my throat. There was no one or nothing in my bedchambers that shouldn't be. My legs were tangled in the single sheet of cotton I used. Part of me wished Luc was here to hold me, reassure me even though we both knew it was a lie.

He hadn't slept in my bed since his child died. Since the night my birth mother plunged her knife into Sister Claudia's womb to use the babe's death to fuel an obscene spell to kill everyone in Orrin and claim the power of their deaths to take over the world. I didn't blame him.

Claudia had visited once. She was now as barren as I was. Master Aaron couldn't replace what the demon magic my mother wielded had corrupted. My meeting with Claudia was awkward. She claimed she didn't blame me. However I blamed myself enough for the three of us.

I unwrapped the sheet from my limbs. There was no point in trying to go back to sleep. A few candlemarks a night was all the rest I could manage before nightmares of my headless mother and Luc and Claudia's bloody babe intruded.

From the silence in the corridor outside my door, we were nowhere near First Morning. Whispers came from the new passage I'd created to the tunnel system, but I ignored them as I climbed out of bed and searched for a loose shirt and loose pants to wear.

Once dressed and my hair tied back out of the way, I padded through the silent Temple. Warden Ahiga nodded as we passed on his patrol, but otherwise, we said nothing. All of the Balance wardens took my idiosyncrasies in stride, just as they did with my fellow justices, Yanaba and Elizabeth.

I passed through the Temple kitchen to the back porch. Our cook Deborah and her kitchen staff weren't even awake yet. The fireplace and the brick oven glowed a dark pink, their fires stoked for the night.

In the exercise yard, I went through warm-ups and stretches before I started on the Jing unarmed combat forms Sister Shi Hua of Light had started to teach me before she also became pregnant.

I went through the first set and started on the second when I felt someone's attention on me. The yellow tomato vines climbing the wooden lattice work of the garden couldn't hide the small figure with the orange face and hands. I frowned.

"Ming Wei, what are you doing up this late?"

Yanaba's squire cautiously peered around the corner of the wood frame. "I couldn't sleep."

"Nightmares?" I asked.

She nodded. The girl had more of a right to bad dreams than any of us. Her parents had sold her to a Jing noble located here in Issura. The noble ill-used her before he burned his manse with himself and his child slaves inside. Ming Wei had been the only survivor.

"May I say something?" she asked shyly.

"Of course."

"You need to keep your back foot pointed forward," she whispered. It was the same weakness She Hua had noticed.

I cocked my head. "You know these forms?"

"Yes, m'lady."

Now, I was thoroughly confused. "Where did you learn them?"

"Mistress Yin Li has been teaching me along with her son."

"During your language lessons?" I gaped at the child.

Ming Wei nodded. "Are you angry, m'lady? Justice Yanaba said it was all right for me to learn and share my knowledge with Nathan."

"I am . . . surprised." And I was. Ambassador Quan and his alleged mistress had been going to the Temple of Light the last few months. Since Shi Hua was a distance speaker, it was easier for them to go there to communicate with the emperor in Jing due to the sister being past the middle of her pregnancy. Of course, the mistress was in fact the ambassador's bodyguard and Shi Hua's maternal aunt. Yanaba had encouraged her squire to relearn the Jing language, something the child refused to speak since the night she was rescued. Plus, Ming Wei's presence would give Yin Li's son someone to socialize with.

"Do you think Mistress Yin Li would allow Nathan to join you for your lessons?" I asked.

"If you asked, I'm sure she would." The girl nodded solemnly.

"Do you think you could assist me with my second level forms?"

Her color brightened, and waves of anxiety rolled off her. "You want me to teach you?"

I shrugged. "Sister Shi Hua started teaching me, but she cannot continue until after her baby is born. I don't want to forget everything she has taught me so far, so I'd greatly appreciate your assistance."

Ming Wei bowed. "I would be honored, m'lady."

Ming Wei and I stopped our practice when the kitchen girls arrived to begin their work. While they proceeded to collect eggs from our henhouse, Deborah stepped out onto the porch and gave Ming Wei a honeyed treat before I sent the child off to the communal bathing room the female wardens used. When I followed my cook and Yanaba's squire into the kitchen, Deborah waited until the child raced down the hallway before she turned, scowled at me, and shook her spoon.

"What are you thinking, Chief Justice?" Deborah waved the spoon dramatically. I was rather thankful she was not waving around a knife. "Keeping that poor girl up half the night! Justice Yanaba actually depends on her squire, even if you don't need young Nathan to the same level."

"I didn't keep her up," I snapped. "I couldn't sleep so I went to the practice yard. She was in the garden watching me, so I invited her to help me work on the Jing fighting forms."

As I talked, Deborah strode over to the cupboard and pulled out left-over sourdough bread and hard cheese. She retrieved a knife and sliced both and placed them on a plate.

"Ming Wei is still having nightmares," I finished softly.

"We know, m'lady." Deborah wiped her hands on her apron before she brought the plate over and gently pushed me toward the table in the little nook her assistants used for prep work.

"Hasn't Yanaba been sending her to Brother Turtle?" I asked. The priest qualified as a miracle worker to me after he saved my junior justice's life when she over extended her spirit in her efforts to save the city from a demon attack last spring.

"Yes, but . . ." Deborah shook her head. "The child has had so much trauma inflicted on her in her short life. Not even Brother Turtle can heal such emotional wounds in half a year."

I nodded and began to eat the bread and cheese. Deborah was right. And I couldn't even begin to comprehend what had been done to Ming Wei, much less how she had the strength to survive it. When I finished, I placed my plate in the tub for used kitchenware.

"I don't know what we'd do without you, Deborah." I hugged the older woman. For the first time, it truly registered how frail she was. She'd been the cook here when my grandmother Thalia was chief justice of Orrin. And I was hardly a child at thirty-one winters.

Deborah patted my hand. "You need a bath yourself, Chief Justice."

I laughed and headed for my quarters.

After bathing and changing, I strode down to my office. My junior justice had been handling court cases, but Yanaba was now halfway through her pregnancy. We'd already lost one potential Light child. Everyone was doting on Yanaba, including me. And it was well past time I began performing my own duties again.

No sooner than that thought had passed through my head when someone pounded on my door. "Chief Justice?"

Warden Mylon's voice. I rarely saw the man. He preferred the night shift.

"Come in," I called out.

He opened the door and peered around the corner. "The magistrate wishes to see you."

Orrin's magistrate Malven DiCook pushed past the warden. Rather than taking it in stride as most of Balance's guards would, Mylon grabbed DiCook's arm and swung him until he was pinned against the wall with Mylon's knife at his throat.

Let's just say there was a reason my chief warden acceded to Mylon's wish for the night shift.

"Anthea?" DiCook squeaked.

"Warden, please release the magistrate," I said. "The duke would be most vexed if you slit the magistrate's throat, even accidentally."

"Yes, Lady Justice." Mylon released DiCook with a scowl. "Next time, wait until you're invited inside." He stalked out of my office and pulled the door quietly shut behind him.

"You're letting your wardens get away with too much," DiCook grumbled as he straightened his jacket. The nights were becoming cooler as we approached the Vintner's Festival.

"And you presume too much, so the contest is even," I shot back. "What are you doing here?"

"Remember Dante and Barbora's shop?"

A chill ran through me. Dante was one of DiCook's top peacekeepers.

Or was until he and his family were murdered to feed the demon eggs planted in their bodies. Dante's wife Barbora ran a seamstress shop, and the family lived in the apartment on the second floor. We tried to locate any family members, but we came up empty-handed, so I signed off on the duchy taking possession of the property to auction off for taxes.

"I thought it was sold at the monthly magistrate's sale."

"It was." DiCook hooked his thumbs in his belt and rocked on his heels. My gut clenched at the sign that I wasn't going to like what I heard.

"The new owner opened up the storefront this morning for the first time." DiCook shrugged. "What she thought was a dead animal inside turned out to be human corpses."

Glossary

Words and Phrases Specific to the Justice Series

Anacapa Islands – a series of four islands off the southwestern coast of Issura. Limuw is the largest. Anacapa is the closest to Orrin.

Apprentice – lowest rank of a trade or craft guild

Britannia – Toscan name for a series of islands off the western coast of the Old Continent. The two largest are Eire and Albion. Four hundred years before Anthea's time, the queens of Eire and Albion were losing their battle against the demons. They ordered the islands evacuated and the Temples of Death to launch their last resort spells. The islands are now barren, and no one who steps on them lives for long.

Briton Diaspora – refers to the survivors and their descendants of the evacuation of Britannia who are now scattered around the world

Brother – title for any fully ordained priest of any Temple that accepts men, except for the Temple of Father

Cant – Issura's neighboring nation-state to the south

Chengzhou – the capital of Jing, a nation-state in the western shore of the Old Continent

Chief Justice – title of the highest ranked priestess at a Temple of Balance

Chief [name of trade] – the highest ranking master guild member of a trade in a city or region

The Cradle – according to legend, the continent where Child created the first members of the human race

Duke/Duchess – highest ranking noble of a region

Distance-view glasses – a telescope

Father – title for any fully ordained priest of the Temple of Father

Gilwas – a city in northern Issura

Gray Mountains – a mountain range that runs the entire length of the western side of the Long Continents

The Grand Canal – a human-built canal that passes through the isthmus connecting the Long Continents

The Green Lady Inn – an inn near the Embassy District of Orrin, it had the only entrance/exit to the tunnel system with the city wall that is not a Temple until it was bricked over and magically sealed after the events of *A Modicum of Truth* and *A Matter of Death*.

Guild – a civil organization for a trade or craft

Guild Master – an expert tradesman's rank based on analysis of his/her peers

Healer – a person with the magical ability to heal illness and repair wounds

High Brother – title of the chief priest of a city Temple, except the Temple of Father

High Father – title of the chief priest of a city's Temple of Father

High Mother – title of the chief priestess of a city's Temple of Mother

High Sister – title of the chief priestess of a city Temple, except the Temples of Balance or Mother

Iberia – nation-state on the southwestern corner of the Old Continent

Issura – queendom on the western coast of Northern Long Continent; the Peaceful Sea forms its western border with the nation of Pagonia to the north, the nation of Cant to the south, the nations of the Cliffdwellers and Diné to the southeast and the Gray Mountains to the east

Jing – nation-state on the eastern side of the Old Continent

Journeyman/Journeywoman – middle rank of a trade or craft guild

Justice – title for any fully ordained priestess of the Temple of Balance; alternate term of address is Lady Justice

Kemet – nation-state on the northeast corner of the Cradle

The Levant – a loose alliance of Phoenician city-states between the Hittite Empire and Kemet on the eastern side of the Middle Sea

The Long Continents – the two continents separating the Peaceful Sea from the Panthalassa Sea, they are connected by a narrow isthmus

The Lost Continent – southern continent between the Peaceful Sea and the Storm Sea. By Anthea's time, the original inhabitants were believed to be slaughtered by demons 500 years before. Sailors from the Sea Peoples and Maurya who landed there after the inhabitants' disappearance reported screams but found no one. Those with magic talents went mad. Not even the priests and priestesses from Child could save them. Those who tried went mad themselves.

Magistrate – elected official of a city or town in Issura who is responsible for civil and criminal law enforcement and the city or town's defense/care in an emergency

Master – senior member of a trade or craft guild; the clergyperson who is primarily responsible for the training of a novice class

Maurya – the southern-most nation of the Old Continent

Middle Sea – shallow sea that separate The Cradle from the Old Continent

Mother – title for any fully ordained priestess of the Temple of Mother

National Road – main, paved road through the nation of Issura. It roughly parallels the western coastline.

New Thenos – an island city/state on the eastern coast of the Northern Long Continent

Novice – a person in training to become a priest/priestess of the Twelve

Orrin – third largest city in the queendom of Issura with the second largest port

Pagonia – Issura's neighboring nation to the north

Panthalassa Sea – ocean that separates the Long Continents from the western part of the Old Continent and the Cradle

Peaceful Sea – ocean that separates the Long Continents from the eastern part of the Old Continent, the islands and archipelagos of the Sea Peoples, and the Lost Continent

Peacekeepers – men and women who act as a city's police force. They report to the city's magistrate. They also act as an auxiliary defense force if their city or nation is attacked.

Pimu – one of a series of four islands off the northern coast of Cant

Rambla – a city in northern Cant, its people were used to hatch demon eggs off-screen during the events of *A Modicum of Truth*

Reverend Father – senior-most priest of a Temple order, the leader of that sect in the nation in which he resides

Reverend Mother – senior-most priestess of a Temple order, the leader of that sect in the nation in which she resides

Seat – person holding the highest ranking position of a Temple

Shakya – nation-state in the western portion of the Old Continent, southwest of Jing and northeast of Maurya

Sister – title for any fully ordained priestess of any Temple that accepts women, except for the Temples of Mother and Balance

Standora – capital and largest city of Issura

Storm Sea – ocean bordered by the eastern part of the Cradle, the southern part of the Old Continent, and the western part of the Lost Continent

Tandor – Issuran city that guards the border with Cant and Diné

Temple – a collection of people dedicated to the service of one of the twelve gods; a building that houses such people; the primary place of worship for one of the twelve gods

Tiwan – the capital of Cant

Toscana – nation-state on the southwest section of the Old Continent; location of the first battle against the demons

The Twelve – the collective name for the twelve deities of the Justice universe

Valencia – duchy in the nation-state of Iberia; know for their innovative shipbuilding designs

Warden – security guard of a Temple, they act as supplementary military personnel in the event of a demon invasion

The Twelve Temples

Mother

Cloak Color – Light blue

Motto – "To give without thought; to forgive with love."

The Temple of Mother is responsible for the teaching of household arts, such as spinning, weaving, food storage and preparation. The order is also responsible for caring for those who have lost their families.

Father

Cloak Color – Dark blue

Motto – "All tools are weapons, and weapons tools."

The Temple of Father is responsible for the constructive arts, such as carpentry and smithing.

Balance

Cloak Color – Black

Motto – "Balance in all things."

The Temple of Balance runs the judicial system. A justice is the judge in criminal and civil cases.

Light

Cloak Color – Medium brown

Motto – "Light brings truth, for without truth, there can be no justice."

The Temple of Light is responsible for codifying contracts and mediating contract disputes. A Light priest also acts as the bailiff for a justice, and is often the one to truthspell a witness or the accused. The Temple of Light also provides military support to a nation's civilian army.

Knowledge

Cloak Color – Gold

Motto – "With patience, knowledge comes."

The Temple of Knowledge is responsible for education and for recording historical events. They essentially act as the library system for the Justice universe.

Thief

Cloak Color – Grey

Motto – "Hiding in plain sight."

The Temple of Thief acts as the intelligence-gathering arm of both the Temples and the civilian leaders. They finance their efforts through gambling dens.

Conflict

Cloak Color – Dark Red

Motto – "Destruction is the necessary evil, for it clears the way for new growth."

The Temple of Conflict focuses on strategy and all martial arts. They are the primary support and teachers of a nation's army.

Love

Cloak Color – Medium Red

Motto – "Pleasure is life."

The Temple of Love are the holy prostitutes. They also deal with sex education and lead the Spring Rituals, the annual fertility rites which were first used to breed as many humans with magical talent as possible. Don't underestimate them. They fight just as hard and as nasty as their fellow clergy in Conflict.

Child

Cloak Color – Light green

Motto – "All things are new once."

The Temple of Child is responsible for the emotional health of citizens. They also develop and teach agriculture and animal husbandry techniques.

Wilding

Cloak Color – Dark green

Motto – "All creatures return to us."

The Temple of the Wildling God deals with management of wild animal populations, forestry, and the protection of ecosystems.

Vintner

Cloak Color – Purple

Motto – "The line between wisdom and madness is one sip."

The Temple of Vintner not only deals with the cultivation of grapes and the production of wine, but they also promote the gathering, cultivation and processing of all medicinal herbs.

Death

Cloak Color – Black

Motto – "For every life, there is a death."

The Temple of Death takes care of the gathering of the dead, the last rites, and disposal of the corpses. They also act as a repository for the last wills and testaments of all citizens.

Characters and Places

QUEENDOM OF ISURRA

ORRIN

Temple of Balance

Chief Justice Anthea – a circuit justice for ten winters until her appointment as Chief Justice of Orrin at the age of thirty winters ("Justice")

Chief Justice Penelope – deceased, predecessor to Anthea as Chief Justice of Orrin

Chief Justice Thalia - deceased, predecessor to Penelope as Chief Justice of Orrin, maternal grandmother to Anthea

Justice Yanaba – junior justice assigned to the city of Orrin after the events of *A Question of Balance*

Justice Erato – junior justice assigned to the circuit of the eastern section of the duchy of Orrin and the southern tip of the duchy of Pana Valley after Anthea is sentenced to the seat of Orrin in "Justice"

Sivan – personal assistant to Chief Justice Anthea and head of the household staff

Donella – senior clerk

Lailani – junior clerk

Chief Warden Little Bear – head of the Balance wardens

Warden Tyra – junior warden, killed in the Battle of Tandor (*A Matter of Death*)

Warden Gina – junior warden

Warden Aglaia – junior warden, died in the battle to retake the Temple of Love (*A Question of Balance*)

Warden Daniel – junior warden

Warden Noko – junior warden

Warden Jonata – junior warden, Aglaia's replacement from the Standora Wardens' Academy

Warden Dezba – junior warden

Warden Tahoma – junior warden

Warden Ahiga – junior warden

Warden Long Feather – junior warden

Warden Ailyn – junior warden, she replaced Tyra after her death

Warden Mylon – junior warden

Hogarth – former chief warden under Justices Thalia and Penelope, now stablemaster, husband of Deborah

Deborah – Head cook, wife of Hogarth

Nathan – squire to Chief Justice Anthea after he was sentenced to pay reparations for stealing bread, an orphan, age ten winters at the time of his sentencing in *A Question of Balance*

Ming Wei – squire to Justice Yanaba, nine winters old at the end of *A Question of Balance*. Originally from Jing, she was sold by her parents to a Jing noble as a sex slave and brought to Issura. When the noble's crimes were discovered, he immolated himself and his slaves. Ming Wei was the only survivor and has severe scar tissue on her face, back and arms.

Temple of Light

High Brother Luc – a circuit priest for twelve winters until his appointment as chief priest at the age of thirty-two winters between the events of "Justice" and "Diplomacy in the Dark"

High Brother Kam – semi-retired, predecessor to Luc as chief priest, poisoned and died during the events of *A Question of Balance*

Brother Mat – Second to Luc. His birth name is Micah. He murdered the real Mat on his way to Orrin from Standora. Died under Anthea's truthspell interrogation in *A Question of Balance*.

Brother Jeremy – youngest junior priest until he is promoted to Luc's second after the events of *A Question of Balance*.

Brother Garbhan – junior priest who is assigned permanently to Orrin after the events of *A Matter of Death*

Istaqa – personal assistant to High Brother Luc and head of the household staff

Edberth – former personal assistant to High Brother Kam, he now acts as evening assistant to High Brother Luc

Henry – stablemaster

Chief Warden Nicholas – head of the Light wardens

Warden Gibb – junior warden, died shortly after the renegades' kidnapping of High Brother Luc in *A Question of Balance*

Warden Mateqai – junior warden, becomes Sister Shi Hua's personal bodyguard during the events of *A Modicum of Truth*

Warden Yar – junior warden

Warden Tadhg – junior warden

Warden Gad – junior warden

Temple of Love

High Sister Gerd – chief priestess, biological daughter of Thalia and Kam, biological mother of Anthea. She was removed from office on charges of fraud, bribery of a public official, unlawful magic, and conspiracy to commit murder. Later, the charges of dealing in demon artifacts and treason were added.

Sister Dragonfly – Gerd's second, *berda* (genderfluid), is acting High Sister after the events in *A Question of Balance*, becomes High Sister after the events in *A Modicum of Truth*

Sister Gretchen – junior priestess, deceased. The discovery of her body in one of Duke Marco's wine barrels precipitates the events in *A Question of Balance*

Sister Claudia – junior priestess, Dragonfly's second

Sister Shada – junior priestess

Sister Zihna – junior priestess

Sister Ilina – junior priestess, Lady Katarina DiMara's mother, she died of the wasting disease prior to "Justice"

Chief Warden Citana – new chief warden of Love after renegades killed and replaced the entire warden contingent of the temple

Warden Jocasta – junior warden, one of the replacement wardens after the events of *A Question of Balance*

Gregorios – a eunuch who was High Sister Dragonfly's personal assistant and head of household until his murder prior to the beginning of *A Twist of Love*

Ichik – a eunuch who is Sister Claudia's personal assistant

Iona – Love's maintenance person, she does minor repairs and servicing of the Temple

Temple of Conflict

High Brother Han – chief priest

Sister Migina – junior priestess

Temple of Death

High Sister Bertrice – chief priestess

High Brother Kai – deceased, predecessor of Bertrice, retired in Bertrice's favor as the temple seat and became a teaching brother in Standora until his death

Brother Xander – Bertrice's second until her demise during the Battle of Tandor, succeeds her as Orrin's High Brother of Death

Sister Raven Claw – Xander's second when he becomes high brother

Chief Warden Axton – head of the Death wardens

Warden Hitari – junior warden

Temple of Vintner

High Brother Ben – chief priest

Sister Nina – junior priestess

Chief Warden Mangas – head of the Vintner wardens

Warden Golden Eagle – junior warden

Temple of Mother

High Mother Bianca – chief priestess, she commits suicide when Anthea discovers Bianca has been selling children

High Mother Leocadia – chief priestess, she transferred from the Temple in Gilwas and succeeded Bianca between the events in *A Touch of Mother* and *A Twist of Love*

Chief Warden Maebh – head of the Mother wardens

Temple of Father

High Father Jerrod – chief priest

Temple of Child

High Sister Mya – chief priestess

Brother Turtle – junior priest, helps to save Justice Yanaba by pulling her soul back into her body during the events of *A Modicum of Truth*

Temple of Wildling

High Brother Jax – chief priest, second form is a wolf

Sister Farrah – Jax's second, second form is a fox

Temple of Thief

High Brother Talbert – chief priest

Sister Cedar Grove – Talbert's second

Chief Warden Sabine – head of the Thief wardens

Temple of Knowledge

High Sister Mariana – chief priestess

Nobility

Duke Benedetto DiMara – father of Marco, Alessa, and Isabella, husband of Cora, convicted of conspiracy and conspiracy for illegal magic to mind wipe his son Marco during the events of "Justice"; imprisoned at Standora for life.

Lady Cora DiMara – mother of Marco, Alessa, and Isabella, convicted of treason and demon dealing, executed by the Reverend Mother Alara of Balance during the events of "Justice".

Duke Marco DiMara – duke of Orrin, inherited his post at the age of eighteen winters after his parents were found guilty of numerous offenses and stripped of their titles and property

Lady Katarina DiMara (nee' DiLove) – common-born wife of Marco, animal healer. Her mother Sister Ilina was a priestess of the Temple of Love and died of the wasting sickness shortly before Katarina's eighteenth winter.

Lord Kam DiMara – eldest child of Marco and Katarina and heir to the Duchy of Orrin, named for High Brother Kam of Light, godson of Chief Justice Anthea and High Brother Luc

Lady Alessa DiMara – sister of Marco, a latent talent, lover of Sister Gretchen of Love

Lady Isabella DiMara – sister of Marco, attends the University of Standora

Bartholomew – retainer of Duke Marco's until it was learned he'd assaulted Lady Alessa and Sister Gretchen, Lady Alessa subsequently asked Chief Justice Anthea for clemency and hired him to manage the estates Sister Gretchen had bequeathed to Alessa

William – retainer of Duke Marco's

Julian – retainer of Duke Marco's

Arturo – former captain of Duke Marco's flagship, his murder is the precipitating event of "Diplomacy in the Dark"

Titus – captain of Duke Marco's flagship, the *Mars Tranquilus*

Citizens

Malven DiCook – duly elected magistrate of Orrin

Dante – one of Orrin's peacekeepers, dies at the beginning of *A Modicum of Truth*

Barbora – wife of Dante, dies at the beginning of *A Modicum of Truth*

Jaime – one of Orrin's peacekeepers

Leyti – one of Orrin's peacekeepers

Drest – a peacekeeper, dismissed by DiCook for extortion

Robin – a peacekeeper, dismissed by DiCook for warning Drest that DiCook was coming to arrest him

Alo – an innkeeper, the owner of the Green Lady Inn near the Embassy District

Chumana – Alo's daughter, she is ten winters at the beginning of *A Question of Balance*

Guilds

Chief Healer Aaron – head of the Healers' Guild

Master Healer Devin – second to Aaron in the Orrin Healer's Guild, originally from New Thenos

Journeywoman Bly – a junior healer, often assists Master Devin at autopsies

TANDOR

High Brother Dav – chief priest of the Temple of Light

Chief Justice Elizabeth – chief justice of the Temple of Balance

Minerva – the new clerk with the Temple of Balance, a renegade, killed during the fight within the Temple of Balance (*A Modicum of Truth*)

High Brother Aduba – chief priest of the Temple of Conflict

Brother Tighan – second of the Temple of Conflict, a renegade, killed by Aduba during the fall of Tandor

High Brother Nantan – chief priest of the Temple of Death

Sister Reby – second of the Temple of the Wildling God, first introduced as a shapeshifting thief in "The Perfect Partner", second form is a polecat

Brother Sisquoc – surviving priest of the Temple of the Wildling God, second form is a panther

Brother Trajan – priest of the Temple of the Wilding God, second form is a wolf

Sister Jumping Mouse – priestess of the Temple of the Wildling God, second form is a kangaroo rat

Duke Enzo DiToscana – Duke of Tandor, murdered by a skinwalker possessing his wife

Duchess Nadine DiToscana – the widow of Duke Enzo of Tandor

Ural DiSand – merchant from Tandor, implicated in the Assassin Guild plots in Orrin, killed while possessed by a skinwalker (*A Modicum of Truth*)

Amarantha DiRoma – Tandorian merchant, rival of Ural DiSand, murdered by renegades shortly before they poisoned most of the personnel of the Tandorian Temples

Govind – a silversmith who assisted with the defense of Tandor against the demon army, settled in Orrin after the evacuation and fall of Tandor

The Wave Dancer – Duchess Nadine of Tandor's flagship, one of two remaining ships in Tandor prior to the Battle of Tandor

STANDORA – capital city of Issura

Reverend Mother Alara – head of Issura's Temple of Balance

Justice Rose – novice training priestess of the main Temple of Balance in Standora when Anthea was a novice

Justice Melanippe – a novice in Anthea's class. She was the top student, but she was also recruited by Thief to report on any wrongdoing in Balance.

Reverend Father Farrell – head of Issura's Temple of Light

Brother Elroy – a Light priest, aide to Reverend Father Farrell, and a distance speaker who accompanies the Isurran and Sea Peoples' fleets to Tandor in *A Matter of Death*

Brother Long Wind – a Light priest and aide to Reverend Father Farrell; he accompanies the queen's army to Tandor in *A Matter of Death*

Brother Garbhan – a Light priest and aide to Reverend Father Farrell; he remains in Orrin during and after the events of *A Matter of Death*

Brother Jon – novice training priest at the main Temple of Light in Standora, murdered by the skinwalker at Samael DiRoy's abandoned manse prior to *A Question of Balance*

High Sister Imala – a Love priestess, considered to be the lead contender for position of Reverend Mother of Love; she accompanies the queen's army in A Matter of Death

Chief Warden Catherine – Imala's chief warden; she was a classmate of Mateqai's at the Warden Academy and the two had a physical relationship

Warden Hototo – a junior Love warden

Brother White Wolf – a senior priest of Thief; he's a personal friend of High Sister Imala

Queen Teodora – reigning monarch of Issura

Crown Princess Chiara – eldest child and heir of Queen Teodora of Issura; lady general of the queen's army

Duke White Eagle – former Conflict brother, left the order to marry Crown Princess Chiara; honorary title duke of Standora as the future queen's consort; lord general of the queen's army

PANA VALLEY

Lord Aleister DeGrove – noble noted for his vineyards

JING EMPIRE

Chengzhou

Empress Bao De – ruler of Jing a century before Bao Yu, she sacrificed herself to stop a demon army

Empress Bao Yu – ruler of Jing until her death from natural causes during "Courting Trouble"

Emperor Bao Chengwu – current ruler of Jing, succeeded his mother Bao Yu during "Courting Trouble"

Ambassador Quan Po – half-brother of the current Jing emperor Bao Chengwu; was heir to the throne until his nephew was born

Reverend Father Jin – head of Jing's Temple of Light

Sister Shi Hua – a priestess of Light, who was tapped as Po's bodyguard. She received additional training from Conflict, Thief, and Love. Originally from the town of Yintze in the southern province of Chu.

Brother Lin – novice master of Light

Brother Jian – a priest of Light, classmate of Shi Hua during their novice years

Brother Fa – a Wildling priest, his second form is a tiger, a friend of Shi Hua and Jian during their novice years

Justice Mei Wen – a priestess of Balance, Shi Hua's closest friend other than Jian during their novice years

Sister Yin Li – a priestess of Love, Shi Hua's maternal aunt

Yin Shang – the son of Sister Yin Li and Brother Shang

Reverend Father Chen – head of Jing's Temple of Conflict

Brother Shang – a priest of Conflict, Shi Hua's instructor when she was a novice

Reverend Father Biming – head of Jing's Temple of Thief

The Unbridled – a spy ship used by the Temple of Thief, a four-masted carrack built in the Iberian duchy of Valencia, captained by Reverend Father Biming during *A Modicum of Truth*

Brother Hadar – a priest of Thief from the Kingdom of Hejaz, serving on board *The Unbridled*

ISLANDS OF THE SEA PEOPLES

Kingdom of O'ahu

Prince Alika – youngest son of the king of the Sea Peoples, one of Sister Gretchen's worshippers, the father of her unborn child

Captain Iakepa – senior captain of the O'ahu trading fleet

DINÉ NATION

Reverend Father Nizhé'é' – head of the Diné Temple of Conflict

Justice Spotted Fawn – the western circuit justice for the Diné Nation, killed in the Battle of Tandor

Bidzii – Spotted Fawn's clerk, he's fluent in Issuran so the justice speaks through him; killed in the Battle of Tandor

Brother Bumblebee – junior priest of Light with the Diné army

Sister Lizard – junior priestess of Knowledge with the Diné army

CLIFFDWELLERS

Healer Kotori – a physician with the Diné army during the siege of Tandor

PLAINS NATIONS – COMANCHE

High Brother Pecos – a senior Conflict priest with the Diné army during the siege of Tandor

Acknowledgments

They say it takes a village.

My village consists of Jaye Manus of QA Productions and Elaina Lee of For the Muse Design for their incredible patience and understanding. Thank you so much, ladies!

My cousin Suzan (yes, there are two of us) for her unflagging support.

And of course, DH for giving into my need for Cinnabons as I finished this book.

Suzan Harden transitioned from writing information technology manuals for companies and legal articles for a law enforcement magazine to her first love, fantasy and science fiction in all their forms. She's the author of the Bloodlines series, the 888-555-HERO series, and the Justice series.

www.ingramcontent.com/pod-product-compliance
Lightning Source LLC
Chambersburg PA
CBHW071528120726
47907CB00013B/1262